# BOOKS BY SKOOT LARSON

## The Lars Lindstrom Zen Jazz Mystery series

The No News is Bad News Blues

The Real Gone Horn Gone Blues

The Dig You Later Alligator Blues

The On the Road Again Blues

## The Dave Holman "Texas" Mystery series

The Texas Detective

The Pachyderm Predicament

## Political Humor

Apollo Issue, a Humorous Look at Healthcare

The Palestine Solution

The Testament of Jessica Crystal

# King Irv's Big Adventure

## A Humorous Fantasy

Skoot Larson

Skoot's Jazz Books

This work is dedicated to Devorah Fox, my favorite writer of Fantasy, her lead character, King Bewilliam, and also to Gene Feldman. The Feldman's were our neighbors when I was a child. Gene was a local school teacher. He taught me to play chess and he introduced me to his Jewish faith. I spent many happy festival days with Gene and his daughters, Amy and Judy, at their temple. Thanks, Gene, wherever you may be. And again, a special thanks to my editor, Theresa Feeser.

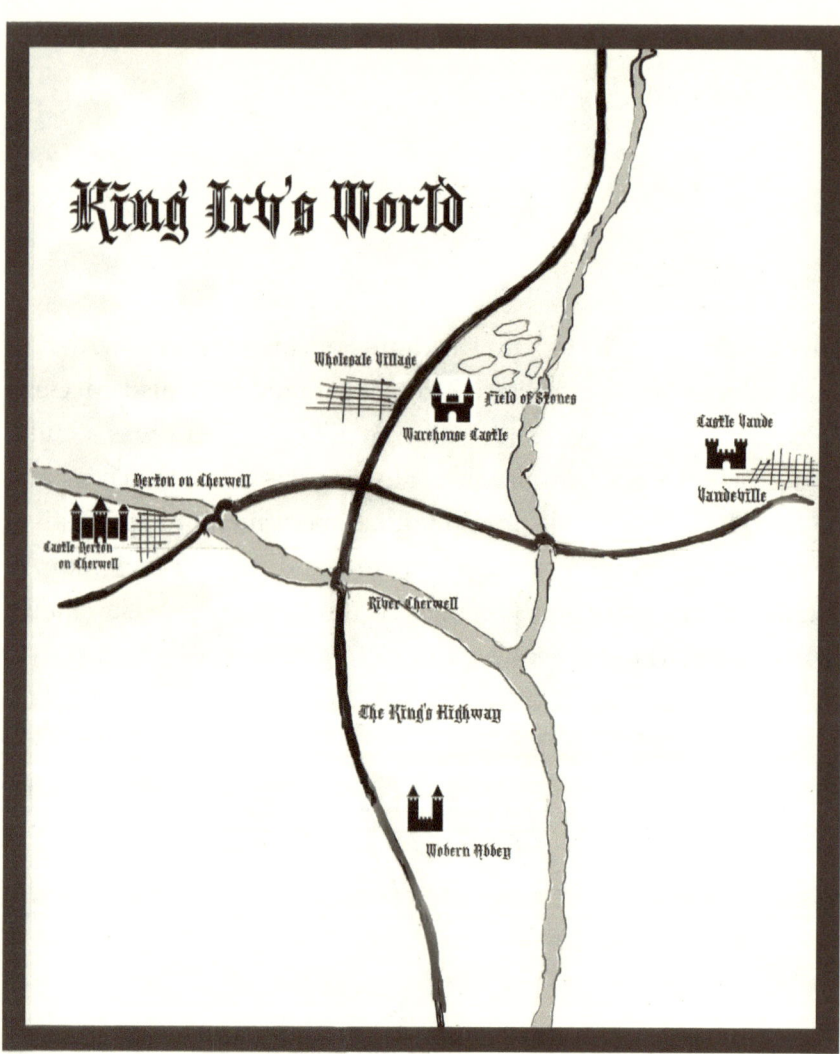

King Irv's World

Wholesale Village

Field of Stones

Warehouse Castle

Castle Vande

Vandeville

Herton on Cherwell

Castle Herton
on Cherwell

River Cherwell

The King's Highway

Wobern Abbey

# Part I

# Good King Irving

## ONE

A tall man with a slight paunch; but regal bearing, dismounted a grey, swayback horse and approached a colorful caravan parked near the edge of a copse of birch trees. The sun shone brightly and the trees were very green. A pair of grey doves flitted about among the branches.

The man wore a conservative gold crown and a crimson tunic. He glanced up at the pennants that waved in the breeze advertising "Dragons for hire." He mounted the three wooden steps and entered the yellow painted wagon through a curtain of colorful beads. A short man with greased-back dark hair, wearing a puffy scarlet shirt and a tiny gold dragon charm in his right earlobe, leaned over the counter and spoke.

"So you want to rent a dragon? You came to the right place. What did you have in mind?"

"Well, something pretty fearsome, I guess. But I *am* on a budget."

"I assume you'll want the fire-breathing variety." The slick little man in the gypsy caravan leaned across the counter, smiled a smarmy grin and wiggled his eyebrows.

"Is there any other kind?" his tall and balding customer queried.

"Yeah, well then, blue flame or orange?"

"Blue flame or orange? Are you kidding me? What's this gesteken?"

"Is there an echo in here? Blue flame burns much hotter than orange, alright? Is this dragon you want to rent gonna have to burn his way through a heavy oak gate or something? Or is the fire breathing just for show? Blue flame will run you about thirty-percent more than the standard..."

"Why is the blue flame more?"

"It's all in the diet. You want a hotter flame, you gotta feed him some temperamental high octane peasants and we don't see a lot of those around here. We have to import them from the southern lands."

"No, no, standard will be fine! I'm looking for a deal here."

"Alright Morris, don't get your jerkin in a twist! So what do you need this dragon for anyway?"

"My name isn't Morris!" the customer proclaimed indignantly. "You should show me some respect here. I happen to be King Irv of the Wholesale Kingdom, in case you didn't notice the crown! I mean, I'm not a stickler for protocol. Like you don't *have* to call me 'your highness' or anything, just make a small show of respect, okay?"

"Oh, I think I might have touched a sore spot here, *your highness*. This dragon you want have something to do with shoring up a failing ego?"

"Well, my ratings as king *are* slipping a bit in the polls..." The king rested his left elbow in his right palm and stroked his left cheek with the other palm. "Even the queen is getting tired of me. All I ever get is dog-style sex!"

"You're complaining about dog-style sex?"

"Yeah. Don't you know dog style sex? I sit up and beg while the queen rolls over as plays dead. A regular princess!"

"And fighting a dragon would be just the thing to improve your standing and maybe your sex life? Where did you say you ruled? The Wholesale Kingdom? I never heard of such a place."

"Hey, it's a great little land, already, and easy to find. We've got fine crafters, smiths, weavers, sword makers, and brewers and in my neck of the woods you'll *never* pay retail!"

"I'll have to check it out some time, if I ever get a few days off from this crummy dragon business," the dark man said with a bored yawn. "Can you imagine feeding these monsters every day and then cleaning up after them? Uff!" The clerk then lit up the full wattage of his smile. "So how did you hear about my little place, anyway?"

"Listen, you don't go looking for dragons on a Camelot."

"Oy, jokes like that, you wonder why you get no respect? So listen, I got a special this week on a medium-sized guy, red eyes and lots of grey-green scales. He's quite a terror. You stand up to this guy its gesament kaputen!"

"And you're sure I can beat him? He'll let me appear to win the match?"

"Listen, your highness, I can rent you a dragon but I can't ask him to throw a match. It ain't legal to fix a fight. You could get me in big trouble with the NADG!"

"The what?"

"National Association of Dragon Gaming. They got a pretty

strong league, you know."

"What, I never even heard of such a thing."

"Obviously your highness doesn't follow the sport. So, aren't you enough of a mensch to stand up to a dragon in a fair fight? I'm on your side, you know. A business like this depends on repeat customers. Where's your chutzpah?"

"Alright, already, so how much? And can I get delivery?"

"Delivery's included, unless you need this beast sent to the outer lands or across a sea."

"No, my kingdom is just on the other side of the dark forest, right off the King's Highway. You know where's that big field of boulders? My castle is just beyond that. So how much?"

"How about twelve gold bars?" the clerk said stroking his chin.

"Twelve gold bars? For a medium-sized dragon with a standard flame? Ach, I'm gonna see you around," the king said edging towards the beaded curtain door.

"Alright, hold on, how about ten gold bars and I'll throw in a horse!"

"I already got a horse," the king shouted, waving his hands about.

The clerk stepped up behind the king and looked out through the beads. "You ride a nag like that and you wonder why you get no respect? Oy vey! Come on, let me put you on *real* horse. I got one that's golden in color. Low mileage too! He was owned by an unpopular wizard that almost never made house calls."

"Okay, ten gold bars. But what am I supposed to do with my old horse?"

"Well, if I had an arrow I could put it out of its misery for you."

"You're kidding me again, right? You're such a kidder!"

"Listen, I was only serious. But if you want to keep him for some reason, I'll loan you a tow rope. He can follow you home."

"You couldn't deliver the horse with the dragon?"

"Are you kidding? Send a small horse with a hungry dragon? I couldn't guarantee that either one of them would arrive! So you got the gold for me?"

## TWO

Back home in Warehouse Castle the sun was getting low in the western sky. King Irv parked his two horses down by the stables where his lazy son, Prince Sol, was sunbathing on a bale of hay, staring empty-eyed up at the passing clouds. Irv cocked his left foot back and gave the straw square a kick to get the lad's attention. "You'd better get up and do some work around here. I want you to brush these horses down, feed them and put some fresh water in their trough!"

The young man blinked a few times, sat up, and gave his father angry eyes. "That is if you have any hopes of borrowing one of these horses to go hang out with you hoodlum buddies on Saturday night."

The boy made some loud, incoherent whining noises but led the mounts inside, pausing briefly to stick out his tongue at his father's back when King Irv had turned away.

The tall monarch decided that since it was such a nice day he should maybe walk around the grounds of his estate and kind of pat himself on the back for all his successes. He breathed a sigh thinking about how much better everything would be once he fought and bested his rented dragon to impress his wife and his subjects. He tried to imagine just what the beast would look like, and more important, he tried to anticipate the looks of admiration his loyal subjects would bestow upon him.

The king's attention was soon drawn to his Merlin who was

furiously riveting pieces of metal together out in the northern pasture. It looked almost as though the man was constructing some kind of oversized mechanical dragon. The monarch quickened his pace over the stony ground. "Hey, Merlin, what are you doing? I just secured us a real dragon!"

"Please, your highness, we've known each other, like, forever. Call me Hershel!"

"Alright already Hershel, so am I right? Are you trying to build some kind of phony dragon?"

The Merlin laughed, "Are you kidding? Does this look like a dragon to you?"

"Well, if not a dragon then what the hell is it?"

"Keep this under your crown, highness." Hershel the Merlin looked all around to see that no one was close enough to overhear them. "It's a *time machine*, your majesty!"

"A what? What the hell is a time machine?"

The Merlin gave more furtive glances toward the trees and then back to the castle. "If my calculations are correct, I'll be able to get into this baby, turn the little dial forward, and I'll step out of it into maybe next year or the year after on this very same spot. Then I'll be able to tell you about what's going to happen… Before it happens! Voilà!"

"Yeah, well don't quit your day job," King Irv told him with a skeptical look. "It would be nice to know what the next year might bring but I ain't gonna hold my breath here. Also, what's gonna power you into the future? Does it take a team of horses or a big fire? What?"

The Merlin bent down and picked up a large square that looked like a giant crystal in a wooden frame. "This is another invention I've been working on, highness," the man stated proudly. "I call it a **sun panel**. This crystal here? It pulls heat from the sun and it changes that heat to power. Limitless power!"

"Okay, you play with your little toy, Hershel. Just be here on call if I need some magic or something. I'm gonna be fighting this dragon I hired when it shows up in the kingdom and I just may need you to put a spell out there or something!"

"Oooow, an enchanting-a-dragon spell. I love a challenge! Don't worry, your highness. I got you covered on that!"

"Thanks, Hershel." The king said patting the man's shoulder. "And you can call me Irving."

## THREE

"How about a glass of wine, my dear?" King Irv had changed into his dark blue smoking jacket with the white ermine trim. His feet were encased in cartoony looking lion slippers, though he still had his crown on his head. The regal head dress, he figured, drew attention away from his receding hairline.

Queen Sophie wore a cotton house dress of teal with a pattern of little gold tiara figures on it that closely matched the one she wore on her head. She was a handsome woman with a nice smile and a ready laugh, although she personally thought that her nose protruded a bit too much. When she was at Torah study as a child, many of her classmates used to rile her up by calling her "Beaky." Her light-weight gold tiara sat comfortably on her dark hair that was starting to go a bit gray around the roots.

"Wine would be nice," she told her husband. "Did you purchase us something exotic while you were out gallivanting around the countryside?"

"We got Concord grape or Thompson seedless," he told her in frustrated tones. They always had to go through this bit of kvetching! "The regular stuff the local guy makes in his old tin bathtubs."

"Oy, I hate living in a wholesale kingdom! Couldn't we move to Long Island or someplace south of the Chalklands?"

"Sophie, what are you saying? We got a great patch of real estate here, alright? The summers are mild and spring is simply gorgeous. Next time I'm out I'll get a case of dago red for you, but I really think we should be buying local, you know? Supporting our own!"

"I'm all for supporting local business, so why don't you plant a better quality of grapes in our vineyard. It's gonna bankrupt the treasury to import a few plants from the southern climes?"

"Lennie, that runs the wine business? He says he isn't sure those expensive grapes will even grow here. We get too much rain."

"Alright, pour me some of the concord plonk. It the only decent vino that Lennie Manischewitz produces for us!"

As they were each finishing their second glass of wine, their daughter, Judith, flew into the chamber red-faced, shaking and crying oodles of tears. Judith was a high-strung young girl of thirteen years, golden hair, her father's green eyes and her mother's easy smile... most the time. She also had her mother's nose and her father's too large teeth in her female parent's small mouth. Sophie constantly begged Irv to look into stories from the west of their land about a Merlin who could straighten teeth by weaving tiny wires around them and rearranging how the pearly whites grew.

"Honey, what's the matter?" Sophie wailed, jumping to her feet.

"Oy, she spoils this child like you wouldn't believe, God," Irv whispered, raising his hands and his eyes toward the high, natural beamed ceiling.

"I ruined the surprise dinner I was making you," Judith hiccoughed with a loud sniffle for punctuation. "I was trying a new recipe for brazed pheasant and I made the fire too hot and now its garbage, charred garbage! And while I was trying to pull the birds out of the fire, all the water boiled out of the pot ruining the brussel sprouts as well. Oh God, I'm such a klutz! You'll probably end up selling me as a slave!"

"Judith, baby. I'm sure it isn't that bad. I *like* my game birds well done." Irv soothed, while Sophie pulled their girl close to her chest and rocked her like an infant with the colic.

Sophie shot her husband an ugly look to tell him she didn't think he was helping the situation. "There, there, darling, we'll have one of the ladies in waiting boil up some rice or something."

Irv rose up from his Lazy-Boy throne and turned to leave the room. "Let me see how bad it is. Maybe I can save the day."

Judith turned her head from under her mother's grasp and gave her father a wan smile of hope. "Thanks, daddy!"

When King Irv returned from the courtyard that led to the kitchens, Judith was occupying his throne and slurping noisily from a large flagon of the Thompson's white wine, which Irv always thought was sweet enough to gag a serpent. The girl's eyes were dry, though still a bit red, and her smile had returned to full wattage.

"So we've got blackened Cajun pheasant," Irv announced, "I basted the birds with some of that hot sauce from the southern lands, and caramelized the brussels. I just threw some butter and sugar in with the greens. It all tastes great, Judith, never mind that it wasn't what you set out to make, it's going to be a really yummy dinner! And I'm gonna eat up every bit on my plate. There's a rumor that a vicious, fire-breathing dragon is headed this way so I'm building up my strength to fight the schtuker if it should show up here in Wholesale land!

"Oh daddy," Judith giggled, "dragons aren't bad! That's just the media trying to control people with fear. Dragons can be just as tame and as lovely as unicorns!"

# FOUR

Irv waited another four days on tenterhooks, anticipating his dragon sparring partner at every turn. His nerves were quickly fraying and heartburn plagued his nights. The heavy footfalls of guards in the hall or the bang of his son kicking a ball against the outer castle wall could almost send him climbing up the heavy wine-colored curtains in the throne room.

Then, just after the Sabbath, on a late Sunday morning, Judith danced excitedly into the library where King Irv was cooling his heels with a bracing tankard of ale.

"Oh daddy? I thought I saw a dragon lurking just across the river. He is so cute! He's got gray-green scales and a fat, forked tail! It's the first real dragon I've ever seen!"

"Ah, a d-d-dragon?" Irv stuttered. "Across our river? You mean like just outside our castle walls?" He gave a little shiver, then caught himself, called on his resolve and put on a brave face. "Guess I'd better go slay it before it can cause any harm to our kingdom. You know how dragons can be!"

"Oh daddy, you don't believe those tales do you? I mean about dragons eating people or roasting things with fire? I think those are just fairy stories! Like those tales about witches and plundering pirates. I'm going to go and make friends with it."

"No! You can't do that, Judith… I mean, you'd better let me go check things out first! I couldn't bear it if you were eaten by a fire-breathing dragon. And what would your mother say?"

"Oh daddy!"

"Oy, I'll bet she'd say a lot more than that!"

King Irv pulled on his tin suit of armor and left the castle, his finest and sharpest sword strapped to his side. He mounted the golden horse that the gypsy dragon-hire man had sold him and cautiously approached the copse of oaks and birches where Judith had indicated she'd seen the beast lurking. There was no bird song, or any other sound for that matter. The landscape seemed quite surreal.

Sure enough, there was the animal he'd contracted for, a regular Godzilla with its scaly reptilian head towering over the trees and his wings beating the still air. When the monster saw him it gave an insolent snort, tongues of flame shooting from its nostrils. Although his body was shaking so bad that the suit of armor he wore sounded like an alarm clock from his bones banging against its insides, King Irv held his head up bravely and advanced.

"Dragon?" he whispered, "Oh Mr. Dragon. Please, God, be merciful with me!" He turned and glanced back at his young daughter who was holding up the hem of her gown and running along behind his galloping stallion. He let his glance drift quickly to the castle. He thought he could make out the frightened face of his wife, Sophie, at the window of her chambers on the second floor as the horse slowed before their quarry. King Irv raised his sword with a bravado he didn't feel as his lips continued to mumble a prayer.

The dragon roared, twelve feet of flame spewing forth, blackening the ground in front of his mount's feet. "How could I be so foolish," he whispered to himself, "and what was I thinking, fighting a dragon, never mind a semi-tame one!"

Wait a minute, did the dragon wink an eye at him? Nich, nich, nich, this couldn't be happening! With a burst of renewed courage, Irv charged forward, chasing the flame-breathing giant back into the thick grove of oak and birch trees. Irv issued a loud war cry. "Rrroa!" he roared, "Rrroa, already!" He got in one good swipe with his sword when the beast stopped and turned.

They were out of sight of the castle now. The animal winked at him again, then rolled over on its back with wings spread behind it and scaly clawed hands in the air. Judith rushed in behind Irv's horse with a cry of "No!"

Seeing that neither her father nor the dragon appeared to be badly hurt, she ran to the fierce-looking reptile and began stroking its lighter green-shaded belly. The dragon had a small slash where King Irv's sword had connected, but it didn't seem to be in any distress.

"See, daddy? He's not so bad. I think he likes me!"

King Irv dismounted and flew to his daughter's side. "Judith," he cried, "What the fuck do you think you're doing?"

"Language, daddy," the girl giggled. "You won the battle, if that's what you were trying to do. I'm impressed, really! I bet mummy will be as well!"

"Not a word to your mother!" Irv sighed, lifting the visor on his tin helmet and wiping sweat from his eyes.

"Oh, daddy! Why do you boys have to play these macho games? Really!"

"Your mother asks, I beat this dragon fair and square! I only spared its life because you begged me to show mercy."

"You got it, pop."

Judith rarely called him 'pop.' A blazing flood of love for his young daughter overcame the king, warming his heart and making him grin.

"And don't say anything to your brother either. Don't tell no one!"

"You mean don't tell *anyone*, daddy. Double negative, but I understand."

 FIVE

Judith followed her father back to the stables where King Irv again interrupted his son's day dreaming to request that he take care of the royal mount; groom and feed the horse. Prince Sol started his usual whine, but then he noticed the small smear of dragon's blood on the stallion's flank. His eyes wandered around the scene, caught sight of the bloodied tip of his father's sword, and flew wide open.

"It was a dragon," his serious-faced sister told him. "Daddy fought it and daddy won!"

"Woe!" shouted Sol, "where's the body. My friends 'gotta see this. My father the dragon slayer!"

"Daddy showed the beast some mercy," Judith told him smugly "He won the fight so what's the point of killing the poor thing?"

"What's the point of fighting a dragon if you don't kill it?" her brother argued. "What kind of story is that to tell?"

"Yeah, I'll bet *you* would have killed it," Judith taunted her brother. "That's just the kind of cold, low-life schtarker you are, you and all your pretend macho buddies."

"Kids!" the king hollered. "I won't have this silly arguing in my castle!"

With a pouting demeanor, Prince Sol led the king's horse back into the stables. Princess Judith began gathering straw and old linen from the stable's tack room.

"And what would you be up to young lady?" Irv asked.

"I'm going to nurse that poor dragon's wounds," she stated with determination.

The beast wasn't hurt bad, but he moaned and faked it pretty well, enjoying the young girl's attention. By evening, the animal came limping out of the forest. There was no fire in his panting as Judith made him a bed of grass cuttings behind the stables and tucked him in.

Sophie's reaction to the fight was mixed. In her heart of hearts she was proud of her brave husband, but she couldn't help kvetching. In her head, she kept pondering the thought that if the dragon had come out the winner, she would have been left alone to run the kingdom on her own. Sure, they had a son who would be heir to the throne, but what kind of a king would a lazy, day-dreaming schtarker of a teenage boy make?

After a couple glasses of the Concord wine, Queen Sophie began to relax a bit. She hooked a hip over the arm of Irv's throne and gave him a peck on his right temple.

"Irv darling, my brave king! I'm sorry I'm such a nag. That was really brave of you, charging out to fight such a huge fire-breathing monster. I love you!"

"So maybe we can go up to the bedchambers for a little, uh…"

"Oh Irv, I just had my hair done and… Oh what the heck, you *did* slay a dragon for me… Okay."

"I *bested* a dragon, Sophie. I wounded it and won the fight…" King Irv gave his queen a lopsided grin, closed his eyes and puckered up for a lingering kiss.

But Queen Sophie was on her feet, tearing at her newly coiffed hair. "You *bested* a dragon? You had the thing hurt and you just walked away?"

"It's okay, babe, everything is cool."

"Everything is *cool?*" his queen roared toward the heavens. There's a wounded dragon out there somewhere and you want me to go upstairs with you like everything is hunky? Irving, don't you realize that a wounded animal is ten, maybe *twelve* time more vicious! That thing is gonna come back and rampage all over the countryside. We're dead meat, you old fool, dead and slightly charred by dragon fire. We just don't know it yet! Do you even *know* where this thing is lurking? You could go out, find it and finish the job!"

"Listen Sophie, it's sleeping out behind the stables…"

"So what are you waiting for? Go kill it, *kill it!*"

"Judith made a nice bed for it out of straw," Irv continued, "its harmless."

Queen Sophie raised her hands to her face and pressed her palms into her eyes. "God? Are you hearing this God? My husband, who by the way has the brains of a headless newt, has left our only daughter alone with a wounded dragon of the fire-breathing variety and he thinks it's time to enjoy a little rumpy-pumpy? Are you hearing this, God?"

Irv got to his feet and tried to take his wife in his arms. "Sweetie," he begged.

"Don't you sweetie me, you serpent!" Sophie wailed. "You, the big brave man who feeds his virgin, teen daughter to a monster! Do we have a suit of armor to fit me? *I'll* go slay the thing. Oy, if you want something done in this world…" And with that, the queen stormed out of the castle.

## SIX

It was a comical scene that met Judith's eyes. She was sitting back, leaning against the outside stable wall stroking her dragon friend's tummy and softly cooing it a lullaby when a creaking, rattling sound filled the evening air. Then her mother, Queen Sophie, was suddenly standing over her, the top half of her father's armor hanging on her shoulders like a sock on a rooster. From behind her back Queen Sophie drew Irv's best sword, took it in a two-fisted grip and tried to raise it over her head, ready to finish off Judith's new pal.

But the weight of the broad sword was too much for the diminutive woman to handle and the weapon continued its arc and tumbled her backwards to the ground.

Try as she may, Judith couldn't control her laughter at seeing her mother sprawled on her back in the mud, her father's chest plate leaning crookedly over the woman's chin. To make matters worse, Prince Sol had heard the commotion and come running with a couple of his buddies. The prince and his friends had stolen a small cask of ale from the pub in the village and burst into drunken cackling of their own upon seeing the queen in such a state. Even the dragon found great mirth in the scene.

Queen Sophie emitted an angry guttural cry as she let go of the blade's hilt and tried to sit up, but soon she was laughing with the rest of them.

"Mummy," Judith announced, "I want you to meet my friend, Burny. That's what I decided to call him, Burny!"

The queen tried to make a serious face, but the whole thing was just too ridiculous and titters kept escaping her down-turned mouth. Finally, she gathered herself enough to speak.

"*This* is the dragon your father slew, er, fought with? This animal you're sitting here petting is the vicious, fire-breathing dragon?" She burst into laughter again, this time holding her sides as tears came into her eyes. When she had composed herself once more, the queen shook her head and said, "This is just like your father, that kook!"

"So can we keep him? Oh please, mummy, I'll take good care of him." Burny the dragon sat upon his haunches and wagged his scaly tail.

"I'll have to think about that one," Sophie told her daughter. "What will the neighbors say? A pet dragon? Oy!"

Judith's pleading eyes locked into her mother's. Sophie's heart began to melt, but common sense was still in control. "Judith, darling, you go upstairs to bed. Stay in the castle tonight and I'll speak with your father about this." The dragon leaned forward, extended an amazingly long forked tongue to lick both the queen's cheeks simultaneously. The beast's tongue was soft and silky. Sophie wiped her face with the back of her hand, but she couldn't help smiling.

## SEVEN

Yes, King Irv agreed with his wife, the dragon was lovable, probably harmless and would make a fairly good pet, but at the same time he was seriously nervous as the dragon was due back at the gypsy's rental place within a fortnight. Would the man be reasonable and maybe sell him the dragon? And if he would, could his small kingdom afford the expense? Oy, how do you explain a royal dragon to the rate payers, a tame one at that? Not even something that could be buried in his defense budget.

Queen Sophie had made a three-hundred and sixty degree turn in her thinking since meeting the creature. Suddenly she was arguing that dragons were basically cuddly and friendly. It was the way people regarded them and treated them that made them nasty and vicious. "Dragons are basically good, kind and loving creatures if treated properly. If you treat a dragon with respect and love," she told him, "you'll get love in return. Aren't they God's creatures just like all the other wild things?" Never mind that a hungry tiger was just as likely to eat you as look at you! When the queen made up her mind that was the end of any argument!

"So, can we do some sort of rent-to-own thing for this dragon?" King Irv asked the slick man in the yellow caravan as he came through the beaded curtains.

"You want to *buy* the dragon? Your ego is going to need some regular boosts in the near future?" the slim, oily-haired man asked him. "Boy, you must be some kind of weak, insecure ruler if you need a staff dragon to be fighting. And have you considered that after a while your subjects are gonna get wise that you're slaying the same dragon over and over, like a bad rerun?"

"Well, it's just that the wife has kind of adopted the guy, you know, like a pet? My daughter's gone and named the thing, named him Burny."

"Now wait a minute, it's not good to go giving a dragon a cute-sy name! A dragon is a wild and vicious beast. Give it a cute name and people tend to forget how dangerous it can be. They put it from their minds that these beasts breathe big flames, they burn down whole villages!"

"Tell it to the wife! She's got this thing eating out of her hand. Ach, you wouldn't believe! And Burny is great at heating left-overs! He breathes on yesterday's meal and it's perfect every time! So what'll you take for him? Can we do some kind of installment plan?"

"Are you bein' real," the gypsy shouted in a rage like fit. "I should be suing the pants off you! What good is a tame dragon to me...? Or anyone else! I can't rent anyone a dragon with no fight in him. To tell you the truth, I'm thinkin' of getting out of this cra-zy business anyway. Either the dragons kill off my customer base, they go soft on me or someone slays my stock animals. Do you know what my insurance costs are every month? I'm hardly makin' ends meet around here. Ach!"

"Yeah, well, how much for the beast then?"

"Keep it, keep the damn thing," the gypsy shouted, slamming his fists on the hard wood counter in his trailer. "I got no use for a tame dragon and I can see I ain't gettin' anymore repeat business outta you. Hell, I don't *want* any more business outta you and your kind! Don't even *think* about referring any of your friends to me! Forget you ever came to my lot or met me! Feekin' idiots!"

King Irv went out through the beaded curtains feeling the dark man's eyes burning a hole in his back. If there had been a door, it would have been slammed hard and locked behind him. On the other hand, he felt great relief. His family would get to keep Burny and he wouldn't have to explain some outrageous expense to his loyal subjects, except maybe the cost of feeding the thing. Just what would it cost to feed Burny anyway? What did dragons eat if not frightened villagers? King Irv mounted the golden horse that had come free as a bonus with his dragon and headed up the King's Highway.

King Irv worried about these things all the way back to his kingdom. In his state of guilt, however, he did remember to stop off at a wine merchant near the old abbey and buy his wife a case of red that the salesman told him had come all the way from Rome. "All my wines come from the southern lands," the man had assured him. Irv wanted to believe the man, but wondered why the merchant's wife's bare feet were stained purple.

Back at Warehouse Castle, the king's family members were having some kind of party in the front garden. There were two freshly slaughtered cows, one on the spit that Burny was roasting with intermittent bursts of his flaming breath, the other that the dragon nibbled at from time to time as he worked. "Well," King Irv thought to himself, "that answers the question of what to feed the thing. I guess we will have to start breading the livestock faster."

Morrie, the court jester, was there with his lute singing a new song he had just composed about Burny the magic dragon. The tall king listened close to the words, but it was all in praise of Burny. There was no mention made of his ever fighting or subduing the beast. "Sometimes I wonder why I even bother," he mumbled to himself as he sat down on the grass.

# EIGHT

With a belly full of roast beef and unleavened bread, King Irv decided he should take a little stroll around the grounds and work some of the calories off. From the mouth of his deep cave in the hillside, Hershel the Merlin waved him over. "Irv, hey Irv, come on over. I wanna talk to you." By the time the king sat down at the small wooden slab in front of the Merlin's cave, Hershel had already poured a couple large flagons of ale for them.

"So, Irv, I got my time machine working!"

"You've perfected time travel? It's really possible?" The king looked his Merlin over in disbelief.

"Possible it is," the man mused with a slightly worried look. "Perfected it's not. By the by, how'd my enchanting spell work on that dragon? Was the thing tame enough for your liking?"

"Ach, that was your doing? It's too tame! Now the wife and kids have adopted the damn thing as a pet!"

"Sorry, Irv. I did my best. I never performed a dragon enchanting spell before. So about the time machine?"

The monarch turned a quizzical face toward Hershel the Merlin.

"So I went to see Rabbi Weise, you know, to kinda get his blessing?" Hershel paused to make sure he had the king's full attention. "The rabbi, he says, 'Hershel, I know you're a headstrong guy, but you know you shouldn't be messing with things like time and space.' He says, 'If God wanted you born in some other time, he would 'a put your parents there and that's where you would 'a been born.' Oy, like he wasn't exactly angry, but he wasn't very pleased with me either."

"Rabbi Weise is a brilliant man, Hershel, maybe you should listen to him."

Hershel took a drink, then gazed off into space. "I don't know… He also says to me, 'What, you wanna pop up somewhere else in history, maybe become a burning bush to somebody? Give'm some kinda bad advice?' I tells him, 'No sir, I just wanna know what's gonna happen, you know, a few years down the line.' The Rabbi tsked me. He says, 'That ain't a very smart thing to do.' Would you believe that?"

"So I guess you'll be abandoning this time travel scheme then?"

"Are you kidding? Abandon what could be a great advancement for science?" Hershel's eyes bore into the face of his king. "So I took the thing for a little test spin this morning."

"You what? You mean you actually traveled through time? Where did you go, what was it like?"

"Well, your worship, you ain't gonna like what I found."

King Irv's full attention was now riveted on the Merlin. He'd almost forgotten the tasty ale that sat in front of him.

"So I land somewhere, I'm not sure what the year is, and your magnificent castle is a ruin, one, maybe two walls still standing, along with the temple. The temple looked in pretty good shape except there was one of those Christian cross things sticking out of the roof."

"This is terrible!" the king exploded. "My castle in ruin? This wasn't, like, real soon in the future was it? I mean not the next year or so?"

"I think it was a *real* long time into the future, your worship," the man said in a low, hesitant voice.

"And stop calling me 'your worship,' will you? I don't mind 'your highness' or 'your grace,' but I thought we were on a first name basis?"

"Sorry, Irv," the man replied. "I guess I'm just a touch nervous relaying this bad news to you. Anyway, when I get out of my machine to have a look around somewhere in the future, all of a sudden these eggs come flying out of the trees, small white eggs, like bird eggs or something, but when they land they don't break, they don't even crack. Next thing I see, four ladies march onto the meadow from the trees. They've got these leather bags slung over their shoulders full of some kinda spears or long arrows."

"Hershel, are you sure of this? Maybe traveling through time made you dizzy or something. Maybe you were hallucinating."

"No, I'm pretty sure I was in my right mind, or as right as my mashugana mind ever is. So anyway, then these ladies start swinging their spears at the eggs, sending them flying…"

"And then did you find out what they were doing, or why they were worrying somebody's hardened eggs?" The king was now very into the tale and curious as to its outcome.

"Well…" Hershel hesitated. "I stepped out for a closer look and one of the ladies went all geshlagan. She's pointing at me and shouting, 'U-F-O! U-F-O!' So the other ladies look up, two of them scream like they're being tortured, and they all start shouting 'U-F-O! It's a U-F-O!' I was in fear of my life, I'll tell you."

So, I guess you won't be going back there again," chortled the tall monarch.

"Au contraire," the Merlin replied. He paused to drain his flagon and then continued, tapping his left index finger against the side of his nose. "I'm planning on going back tonight, under cover of darkness. I'll bring a torch with me and have a good reconnoiter around."

"Is that wise?" questioned the king.

"Hey," Hershel replied, "there shouldn't be a lot of people wandering around the meadow at night. I think I'll be safe."

## NINE

His meeting with Hershel the Merlin left King Irv with mixed feelings. How had his castle been destroyed and how far in the future? And a cross atop their temple? Should he be doubling the guard to watch out for those Christian kings in the district that might attack Warehouse Castle?

Between Hershel's strong ale and the big meal he'd eaten, Irv was a bit sleepy. He decided to go up to his chambers and catch a short nap. Or maybe he was already napping and had dreamt all this craziness?

He was awoken by Queen Sophie, who must have come silently into his room, taken off her clothes and crawled under the linen sheets beside him. Or maybe he was still dreaming?

His wife was kissing his neck, blowing hot breath in his ear. Her hands traveled all over him. Could this be true? "I love you, Irving, you big mashugana," She whispered in his ear as she threw a leg over his quickly rising mensch-hood. "You're completely crazy, but you're such a *good* man! And a good father!"

Those were the last word she spoke before they both surrendered to a passion like the tall king hadn't known in how long? His queen was all over him. He was thrilled and delighted. This is the way it should be! Maybe he should bring home more wine and dragons if this was the result.

When Queen Sophie rolled off of him he was totally spent. She snuggled tightly into his side. "Irv, my love, did I remember to thank you for the wine? And the dragon?"

He could find no words to answer her. Yes, King Irv was in heaven! The dragon, the wine, it was all money well spent. He should have given more thought to pleasing his queen like this years ago! Ah, but years ago, it was more often than not like this... When they were young and courting, oy what memories! And now his life was getting back on track.

"Sophie, oh, Sophie!" he breathed just before he dozed off again.

When he awoke, he was alone in his large canopied bed. The mullioned windows showed that it was dusk outside. There was a little bird song, but no other sounds to disturb the lovely evening. King Irv thought about just rolling over and going back to sleep, but knew if he did he would be up before sparrow's fart and it would be a long day indeed. So he hauled himself out of bed, pulled on some suitable royal attire and decided to go to the village pub and mingle a bit with his loyal subjects.

It was a Tuesday evening and the place was crowded. There were the regulars, of course, and a sprinkling of travelers seeking shelter for the night on their way to Londres, Yorke or other destinations. The king ordered a tankard of the establishment's best ale and retired to his customary table in the corner by the front window. A buxom barmaid, not much older than his own daughter, Judith, brought his drink, curtsied and said, "Bless you, your highness." Irv gave her a brass coin and a big smile.

As he was wiping his mouth from his first large swallow, the landlord came out from behind the bar, looked around and hurried towards his table.

"Ah… Good evening, your highness…" he began.

"And a gracious good evening to you as well, sir," King Irv smiled.

"Well," began the landlord, "not as good as all that. I'm sorry your highness, but I must protest. That loudmouth son of yours has been pilfering small kegs of ale from my back porch again! I know it's a whole gang of these boys that are having a free party with my drink, but they're having your little prince do the dirty work and then they're hiding behind him and his social standing, like I can't say anything! And to make matters worse, your boy is bragging about how easy it is to steal from me. I'll tell you, this isn't doing wonders for either of our reputations, yours or mine!"

The king frowned. "I'll have a word with that boy. I promise you, it won't happen again!"

"Problem is," the pub owner continued, "these kids today got too much time on their hands, especially the rich ones, if you'll excuse my saying."

"So, can I pay you for your loss?" Irv enquired.

"I'd rather you made your privileged little ponce of a prince come in and pay me himself. Or better yet, he can spend an afternoon carrying firkins up from the cellar and washing dishes for me. I think that would be better. Make him understand that some people have to carry their own weight in this world, no offense to you, your highness."

"I totally agree," the king told him. "I'll escort young Sol around here myself on the morrow. And if I can, I'll try and get some of his hoodlum friends to join the work party. Anything more physical they might help with? Cleaning drains or painting walls?"

"Thanks, your highness. I knew you'd understand… And your drinks are on the house tonight!"

## TEN

King Irv was up early the next day. He had a big breakfast of duck eggs and fried tomatoes to build up strength for the coming encounter with Prince Sol. He wasn't about to let one of his own make an embarrassment of him in his local village! He walked out into the meadow to search for the lad while rehearsing the dressing down he would give the boy when he found him.

The prince wasn't sunbathing by the stables and he wasn't bouncing his ball against the castle wall. Then, from the far side of the glen, by a small hill, he heard Hershel the Merlin calling his name. Irv sauntered over toward the man's cave, where Hershel seemed to be sorting through a large pile of junk resting beside his time thingy.

Getting closer, the king thought he saw a dead body among the debris. Sure enough, Hershel was undressing an average-sized man with long greasy blond hair. Beside the body there were a couple of square, flat boxes, a pile of metal cylinders and a few round and dimpled eggs.

"Help me get this guys boots off, would you please, sire?"

"What the Fu… Hershel, what's going on here? Who is this guy and what's all this other stuff?"

"It's a long story, Irv. Help me get this guy undressed and I'll tell you about it as we work." The Merlin had pulled the man's boots free and was pondering his next move.

The king bent down for a close examination of the junk Hershel had resting on the grass by his machine. He tried to pick up one of the cylinders. It was heavy and attached to three other tubes by some kind of stretchy material. The front of the thing said 'Mann's Strong Ale' on it. The large squares boxes had been fashioned from heavy bits of paper and bore the word 'Pizza.' He knew what strong ale was, but what the hell was pizza?

"Your highness, do you mind? Are you gonna give me a hand here?"

Hershel had the belt and fly undone on the body and was trying to wiggle the dead man's trousers down. "If you can grab this guy's cuffs and pull, I'll lift up his fat butt."

The king looked on in amazement. "This guy is dressed really strange," he said. "I've never seen cloth like this!"

"That's 'cause he's from the future," Hershel told Irv with a straight face. "I must have landed my time machine on him and broke his neck. So will you help me get his clothes off or not?"

The king grabbed the strange, plaid-colored trouser legs, one in each hand and pulled them off the corpse.

"Thanks," Hershel barked, taking the pants from King Irv's hand and holding them up against his own torso. "I think these will just about fit me. I'll have to cinch the belt up a bit…"

"Wait just a cotton pickin' minute, Hersh, are you nuts? You want to try on some dead guys pants?"

"And his shirt too," the Merlin answered. "I already checked the hat and it has a little belt in the back you can adjust to any size head."

"The hat?" Irv looked confused until Hershel reached behind him and brought out a funny beanie thing with a sun shade attached to what he guessed was the front. The cap was forest green with gold letters sewn on the front that said 'Castle Golf Club.' What the hell was a golf club?

Irv picked up one of the eggs. It was round and had little dimples all over it. Someone had written Maxfly across the egg in a very precise hand.

"Stop, Hershel!" the king barked. "Cease and desist at once, don't touch another thing until you explain this to me. What are these things…Who is this man? And why do you want to wear his ridiculous suit of clothes!"

Hershel sat back on the grass with a huff. "Alright, your highness, but maybe we'd better have a drink while I tell you about what happened."

"That bad?"

"Right now, I can't say if it's bad or good. It just happened." Hershel reached over and freed one of the heavy cans that said 'Mann's Strong Ale' from its binding. He turned the thing over in his hand, checking all around it, then found a little tab thing attached to the top. Shrugging his shoulders in a 'why not' gesture, he pulled on the tab, which made a slight hissing sound and a burst of foam shot out. When it stopped fizzing, Hershel shrugged again, held the metal tube over his face and poured some amber liquid into his mouth.

"Not bad, your highness, you want to try some?" Hershel freed another of the cylinders, popped it open and handed it to the king. "Ale from the future," he smiled. "It seems to travel okay."

The king took the proffered canister and ventured a tiny sip, then took a longer pull of the future ale.

"Okay, Hershel, so they got ale in the future, and it ain't bad, now please tell me how it got here, will you?"

## ELEVEN

Hershel rolled the ale can, which was surprisingly cool, back and forth along his forehead, then leaned back against the side of his time machine and began his story.

"So, I told you I was gonna go back after dark to have a look around this place in the future, where your castle was fallin' down? Well, that's just what I did. I set my controls exactly the same as before, and I had to use this other invention I've been working on, a clay jug with some acid and a tin rod in it that stores power from my sun panel, I call it my sun jug, but that's another story.

"So I fire up the old machine and I'm off. It was nearly a full moon, so there was lots of light to see by. Next thing I know I feel a strong thump. I look out the machine's portal and there's a couple guys shouting, just going nuts right outside my door. They're screaming, 'Freddie, what happened to Freddie?' Who's Freddie I'm thinkin', then I look down and see this guys feet stickin' out from under my time machine."

"That must have been Freddie," King Irv stated the obvious.

"Yeah, probably," Hershel mused. "This is most likely Freddie layin' right here without his trousers. So anyway, I step out of my vehicle and the other two drop what they're holding. One had these tin tubes of ale clutched in his hands; the other one was holding the boxes. They stop shoutin' about Freddie, throw their hands in the air and bellow something like, 'It's a fair cop, Gov.' But I was more concerned about the guy sittin' under my machine. I eased his body out from under the skids and start apologizing for landing on him. 'I'm not real experienced at this thing yet, you see,' I told the dead man. 'I haven't figured out just how to steer it. And besides, how could I have known you'd be right here in my meadow?' I patted his cheek a time or two to bring him around, but his head lolled over at a real bad angle. That's when I realized he was dead. I must have snapped his neck."

"Not a good way to make friends in the future," Irv told him shaking his head.

Hershel took a sip of ale and continued his tale as if the king hadn't spoken. "One of the others, standing there with his hands up, shouts, 'He ain't no copper, let's leg it,' and the pair took off running into the darkness. So I picked up the boxes and the cylinders and put them into my time machine. I figured it probably was a bad time to explore once again. Those two could return at any time with other men to avenge their buddy Freddie."

"Good thinking," agreed the King, reaching for another of the strong ale cans. "By the way, this future ale isn't bad stuff."

"So I'm pondering my options," Hershel went on. "Maybe I should take this dead guy back with me, I might be able to learn something. Also, if I came back to the future wearing Freddie's clothes, as long as I didn't run into his two mates, I could pass for one of these future people and ask some questions about what happened to your castle, Irv. Know what I mean?

"So, as I'm pullin' his body all the way free, I notice he's got a death grip on the handle of this large metal case with little wheels on the other end. It's resting just behind the skids on my time machine. Like I said, the dead guy still has one stiff hand wrapped around the handle of it and I'm gettin' real curious. I loaded Freddie and his tin case into the machine with the cans and the boxes. The case is really heavy, like I almost get a hernia pickin' it up! As I'm straining to lift the big metal case, I stepped on something that almost sends me flyin'! That's when I noticed these little eggs on the grass. I surmised that they were the same tough little eggs the ladies had been whacking with their spears earlier on, so I loaded them up as well and I fired up my time machine thing to bring us back here."

"So, have you figured out what pizza is yet?" Irv inquired.

"Tell you the truth, I haven't gotten that far," Hershel said scratching the crown of his head. "Let's check it out."

King Irv lifted the lid on one of the boxes to find a round and flat bread-like thing resting in the square of pasteboard. It emitted a very pleasant smell and it seemed to be cut and separated into long triangles. He tipped his head toward Hershel, "May I?"

"Go right ahead, your highness," replied the Merlin.

King Irv took a small, hesitant bite from the point of one of the triangles. "Oy, my God!" he exclaimed. "That is tasty!"

Eyeing the monarch's ecstatic expression, Hershel the Merlin popped open another ale and grabbed a slice of his own from the box. "Yummy!" Hershel agreed. "I can taste tomatoes, some kind of cheese, fish, and there appears to be some mushrooms melted into the cheese. This is fabulous!"

"Do you mind if I take the other, uh, I guess you call this bread thing pizza, mind if I take the other box back for Judith to sample? She's experimenting a lot in the kitchens these days. Maybe she can figure out how to make these things? Then we could have them anytime we want with our ale!"

"Brilliant idea, Irv! And I hope she can get it in a hurry. I'm gonna be craving more of this stuff, and soon!"

## TWELVE

King Irv presented Judith with the pizza. He told her only that Hershel the Merlin had 'found' it and they had both agreed that it made a tasty snack. "Do you think you can make something like this?" he asked his daughter.

The Princess sampled some of the bready dish and squealed with delight. "Yes! Oh my! Thank you, pop. Yes, I will have to figure out how to make this. I simply love it, it's so delicious!"

"By the way," Irv asked his daughter. "Have you seen our little prince anywhere? I can't seem to find him."

Princess Judith pulled a face. "He's out in the woods with those nasty friends of his, Rowland and Baldric. He said they were planning to kill sparrows with their slingshots. That is just so not right!"

"Ah, I'd like to have a few choice words with all three of them. Did he say which woods?" Irv further inquired.

"I think they went west, across the highway. Daddy, can't you make them stop doing such evil things? I mean, what have the sparrows ever done to them?"

"Exactly!" exclaimed the king, pivoting on his heels and heading for the door.

King Irv set out through the oaken forest across the highway from his castle. Small lizards watched from the rocks along the trail and the eyes of foxes and raccoons peered from behind bushes of basil, rosemary and mint. King Irv found the boys crouched down behind a stout rock about a half mile beyond the King's Highway. The three all had their home made weapons in their hands. There was a small pile of pea-sized gravel between them but, as far as the king could see, no dead birds as yet. The trio was so focused on a half dozen small feathery song birds occupying branches in front of them that it was easy for the tall monarch to sneak up behind them.

Prince Sol had his slingshot loaded and cocked, his pink tongue showing at the corner of his mouth in concentration as the king clapped a hand on his shoulder and shouted, "Alright you. We need to have a little talk and right now!"

The pebble from the prince's weapon fired harmlessly, shredding some leaves in a nearby live oak tree. "What now?" whined young Sol. "Can't I have any fun?"

His mates, Baldric and Rowland, rose to their feet and started to back away. "I, ah, I think I hear my paw calling me," Rowland mewed in a soft voice.

King Irv made his voice loud and commanding. "Not so fast! Both you lads stop. Stay right where you are!"

Baldric looked up unsure. Could they outrun the king? And would they be in more trouble if they did try to get away?

"As your king, I command you both to sit back down, right here beside *Prince Sol*." There was disgust in the way Irv said his son's name.

"My dad said we could hunt for birds," Baldric offered in a cocky tone.

"This isn't about killing birds," the king bellowed. "This is about stealing property that doesn't belong to you. You know the

Torah says 'thou shalt not steal.' It's a sin, and it's also not very nice."

The boys turned up their faces with looks of doubt and confusion. "Stealing? We ain't been stealing anything," Prince Sol whined.

"How about kegs of ale from Mr. Miggin's public house? Somebody has been stealing drink, and I've found an empty or two not far from our own Warehouse Castle stable!" His unrelenting eyes bore into the trio of boys. The lads said nothing and tried to muster up some bravado until Rowland's lower lip began to quiver. "It was all Sol's idea," he wailed.

"Not so," mumbled Baldric. "You're a dirty no-good rotter!"

"Aw, pop," Sol wailed. "It was just a bit of fun. We didn't mean no harm, honest!" He tried a sorry smile on his father.

"And it will not happen again?" the king queried. "You had better promise me that."

Three heads bobbed affirmatively in unison. "So now, how are you going to make this up to Mr. Miggins?" Irv asked them.

"Make it up," the prince parroted, "What do you mean, make it up?"

"Well, as I see it you owe him for the ale you drank and the kegs you took to get that ale, which are not only his property, but also a tool used in running his business. So now, how can you make this up to him?"

"Like, you mean we have to meet him, like, face-to-face and admit that we took his stuff?" the prince replied, on the verge of tears.

"That is precisely what I mean," smiled King Irv. "I'm a little thirsty right now myself. Why don't we all march over to the village and you can make your peace with the landlord while I have a tankard of his best."

The boys all wore crestfallen looks, but no one dared disobey their monarch, least of all his own son. They marched ahead of the king, single file right up to the village pub and through the door, where they doffed their caps before Mr. Miggins.

The landlord gave King Irv a broad grin. "Well, well, what do I have here, some workers volunteering to help me out?"

The boys studied their toes, shifting their weight from foot to foot.

"And just in time," the landlord continued. "The septic out back seems to be backing up on me. I wasn't looking forward to clearing it out myself."

A collected groan came from the three lads. They looked back at King Irv as if expecting they might get a reprieve, but the monarch kept a stern face and told them, "You know what you have to do, boys."

Mr. Miggins marched the boys out the back door. The young bar maid from the previous night smiled from behind the bar. "His lordship said you might need a drink while waiting for your lads to finish. It'll be on the house, to show daddy's gratitude for you setting things right."

"I was planning on heading back to the castle to see to a few things," Irv began. "But I wouldn't want to offend by looking askance at the landlord's hospitality." He started for his usual window table and the girl followed with a large, litre-sized mug.

# 🐉 THIRTEEN 🐉

King Irv returned to his castle that afternoon to find his daughter, Judith, very upset. She was sitting on a three-legged stool in the kitchen crying. "Oh daddy, I've been trying to create pizza, but our ovens just don't get hot enough to melt the cheese or properly bake the bread. I've made a disaster of everything. You'll probably want to sell me as a slave."

"Judith, honey," he said trying to comfort her. "You've only just started. You can't give up yet. What has it been, five hours? You're only just beginning to figure this out. Let's think this thing through. Tomorrow's another day."

"That's easy for you to say, daddy. What do you know about ovens and heat?"

"Judith, darling, get out of the kitchen for awhile, do something else to take your mind off it. I'm sure there's a reasonable answer and it will come to you. Why don't you go have a glass of wine with your mother?"

Judith tried to give her father a positive smile. "Okay, daddy. I'll try."

Thinking about pizza, King Irv remembered that Hershel probably had a few more slices left, and more of the good future ale, too. Irv decided to go back to the Merlin's cave and check how things were going.

He found Hershel sitting on the ground outside his cave, staring into a deep pile of fancy paper squares covered with pictures and writing. "So what is this, now?" he asked, parking his own butt on the grass alongside Hershel. "Did these fancy papers come from the future, too?"

"They were in that metal case with the handle and the wheels," Hershel told him without looking up. "They aren't coins, but the writing on them says that they're sterling silver, hundreds of pounds of silver for each piece…"

"Hersh, maybe you better back up and tell me the story from where we left off before I took the other pizza to Judith. By the way, is there any of that pizza left? Or any of the future ale?"

"There might be an odd slice of pizza, look in the box over there. I know there's more ale, why don't you open a couple cans for us."

King Irv opened the pizza box finding just a couple stale crusts. He scarfed them down then turned to the ale cans. There were three left in their stretchy holder, so he pulled out two, popped their tops and gave one to Hershel.

The Merlin shook his head and blinked his eyes. "Okay, where did we leave off?"

"I took one of the boxes of pizza to Judith. You were trying on the dead guys clothes…"

"Oh, yeah," Hershel said, "before I tried to open the metal box which, by the way, was no simple task. I knew that it had to open up, because it had what I recognized as these tiny hinges on the side, but what I guessed were the locks had the tiniest keyholes I've ever seen. I tried to pick them with a bit of wire, but no dice, so I got out a hammer and chisel and I started whacking the side by the hinges. The hinges busted, but the top still didn't want to come off. I had to knock a wedge under the top and pull really hard until the lock thingies busted."

"But it looks like you got it open," Irv ventured.

"Yeah, after an hour or more of struggle," Hershel sneered. "Anyway, at first, I see all this paper and I says 'oh shit, I worked hard for this?' But then I decided to take a closer look."

"So what is it? You said it's paper made of silver?"

"No, not *made* of silver, your highness. Near as I can figure it's like some kind of I.O.U.s that a person can turn in to *get* silver. My guess is that maybe in the future things cost so much you couldn't carry enough gold or silver around with you, so you give the bar maid at the pub or the other merchants these bits of paper and later they can go to the local king and redeem them for the silver. Or something like that."

"Wow," the monarch whispered in amazement. "You think it gets that bad?" He swallowed the last of his can of future ale and reached for another one. "Oops, looks like this is the last one, mind if I take it?"

"Enjoy, Irv, I'm going back tomorrow to try and get some more. Maybe I can get us more pizza too. And hopefully, I can find us some answers."

"Hershel, is that wise? Last night you killed a man there and tomorrow you want to go back?"

"Well, Irv, I've been thinkin' about it, those guys, including this Freddie that I killed? I think they were bad guys, that they were up to no good. I just kinda got that feeling. So if I put on these future rags, I'll be able to talk to some people there. Oh, and I'm gonna move my time machine real close to the mouth of my cave, so I won't end up right in the middle of the field where all those eggs are flyin' around."

The king extended his right hand to Hershel. "Well, old friend, it's been nice knowing you…"

"Irv… *Highness*, don't worry! I'm gonna be just fine. I can handle myself pretty well. And I'm probably smarter than some bunch of people that chase eggs with sticks. What kinda people do something like that for fun?"

# FOURTEEN

King Irv slept fitfully that night. He was concerned for his friend Hershel, who didn't have enough common sense to keep away from the crazy future where people drank ale from tin cans and chased eggs with sticks. He worried about his son who didn't have any ambition and just wanted everything handed to him. And he felt for his poor daughter who got upset so easily.

It must have been close to dawn when he finally got a good hour or two of rest. And the sun was shining high and bright in the sky when his slippered feet finally hit the cold tiles of his bedchamber floor. He stumbled down the back staircase to the dining hall where he summoned one of the servants to see if there was any breakfast left in the kitchen.

The servant seemed to be taking his sweet time, where was he? But instead of the man he'd sent out, his daughter, Judith came bounding into the chamber shouting "Ta-dah!" and setting a small, hot pizza pie on a silver platter in front of him. It was cut into slices, just like the original.

"Oh, daddy, you were right, you are so smart!"

"Huh," the still dozy king said, "What? How was I right?"

"You said to just give it some more thought, like about how to make pizza? By the way, try that and let me know what you think. Is it yummy or what?"

The monarch dutifully picked up a slice of the pie and bit off a hunk, chewed and gave a satisfied "Ummm!"

"Oh, pop, I love you!" his young princess exploded, leaning over to give him a hug around his shoulders and neck.

After chewing thoroughly and swallowing, King Irv said, "So how did you do it? How did you get the ovens hot enough?"

Judith giggled. "Didn't need the ovens, daddy! You always say use your brain, so I took a glass of wine out to the stables to sit with Burny while I was thinking… And it suddenly came to me! What could be hotter than the royal ovens? A dragon's flame! I brought my pizza ingredients out to the field, made up a pie on one of those flat boulders… And I had Burny breathe fire on the side of the rock until the crust started turning golden brown and the cheese melted! It was so simple, really."

"And Burny didn't mind?"

"Daddy, Burny and I adore each other. He's happy to do any-thing that pleases me, though I *did* have to feed him an extra cow to keep the heat up in his flame."

The King chuckled. "So now, thanks to my brilliant daughter, we can have pizza whenever we want. Can I share a little of this with you?" He motioned the princess to the bench beside him.

"Oh, daddy, I couldn't. I'm positively stuffed! Sol and I just wolfed down three of these pizzas." Then seeing the funny look her father gave her she said, "Uh, just to test them and make sure they were okay before offering them to anyone else."

"So your brother likes the stuff?" Irv asked his princess daughter.

"I think so, but he was kind of distracted. He was drawing something that looked like a battlement on a big piece of parchment. Boys!" Princess Judith shook her head in disgust.

King Irv decided he should check up on his son to see just what the young man was up to. He found the prince at one of the outdoor tables where they occasionally dined when the weather was clement. Sol was leaning over a square of thick paper with a piece of gray chalk, his face bathed in concentration. The chalk lines drawn on the page did indeed look like some sort of battlement with a wide portal at its center. It depicted thick timbers stuck into the ground and held together by smaller cross beams lashed to each of the logs. A fat lintel sat over the center opening.

"That looks pretty good, son," the king told him. "Are you designing a castle of your own?"

Without looking up from his work, the lad said, "It's a dragon enclosure, a big one that can make Burny invisible from the highway."

"And is there some reason we need to hide our dragon?" Irv inquired. "Has someone complained about the sight of him?"

"It's gonna be a roadside attraction," Prince Sol answered. "I'm gonna make Burny a roadside attraction." He went on with his sketching.

"And just what, dare say, is a roadside attraction?"

"It's an attraction at the side of the road," the boy whined. "Something people going along the road will want to stop and look at!"

"Maybe you could explain better, I'm not sure I'm understanding this." King Irv said, parking himself on the bench across from the boy.

Prince Sol made an exaggerated show of putting the chalk down and turning his head up to face his father. "You keep sayin' that I got no ambition and that I should find something constructive to do with my time. So I got this idea to do something. I'm gonna set Burny up as a *roadside attraction*.

The king nodded for the boy to continue.

"Well, you see," Sol paused, searching for the right words. "How many people have ever seen a dragon up close? Everybody is always *talking* about dragons, but whoever gets a good look at one? I think people are really curious to *see* one, but they're afraid to go out and get close to such a beast."

"That's pretty sound logic," the king agreed. "I think people are always interested in things that frighten them."

"Yeah, right, dad. So me and Row and Baldric, we're gonna start a business to sell people a chance to get close to a dragon, without being afraid they're gonna get burned and die. Judith says we can use Burny." The prince cocked his head at his father as if asking permission. When the king nodded his head in the affirmative, Prince Sol continued. "We're gonna build this enclosure, the wooden front part is what I'm drawing here, so we'll know just what to put up and then we'll construct smaller fences behind it, to separate Burny from the people that pay to see him. I'm thinking we can probably ask for a brass coin from each traveler at the gate and we'll make enough that we can help you feed Burny with some brass left over that we'll be able to buy ourselves ale and not steal it! Brilliant, huh?"

"Well, I'm not sure boys of your age should be consuming too much ale… But the basic idea is good. Burny *does* tuck away a fair amount of beef every day, and I like the idea of you doing something positive with your time instead of just loafing around…"

"So you'll help us to build this thing?" the young prince asked, his voice full of enthusiasm.

"I'll tell you what," the king said with a hard look. "I'll have a couple of my woodsmen cut the trees for you and I'll provide one of the castle carpenters to oversee the project. But you boys will have to do the hard labor of building this enclosure. That will prove to me that you're serious about the idea. And I'll wish you lots of Mahzel!"

Prince Sol smiled a rare broad smile without a hint of brooding in it. "Thanks, pop! You're the greatest!"

## FIFTEEN

From the interview with his son, King Irv strolled over the meadow to Hershel the Merlin's cave. He found the man staring disgustedly at two large piles of cylinders, like the ones the Mann's Strong Ale came in. Some of the cans were crushed or dented. A few of them bore the Mann's Strong Ale wording, but others had strange words on them like Budweiser, Watney's, Guinness and John Courage. They all appeared to be empty.

"Another fine mess!" Hershel lamented.

"What happened?" asked the curious monarch.

Hershel kicked at the pile of cans, sending a few flying. "I decided I'd make another trip out in darkness. I was thinking I could better orientate myself to the future land before I started trying to chat up these future people, you know? No sense going there looking like some kinda lost hayseed."

The king stared at his friend, remaining silent.

"So I go for a little walk-about. Just the other side of one of your remaining castle walls, there's this little cottage. It's got a sign over the door says 'Clubhouse' and another entrance at the side with a plaque that say 'bar.' I know what a bar is, so I try the door, but it was locked. Next I take myself behind the area that's supposed to be the bar. There, I find these weird transparent sacks labeled 'recycle.' I take a closer look, and I see the things are full of ale cans."

"And you drank up all this ale already? And you're still standing?" The king was amazed.

"Yeah, I wish!" said his friend. "I'm thinkin' we'll have plenty of good drink for awhile, when I hear approaching footsteps. I turn around and some fat guy all dressed in gray with a big patch on his left breast that says 'Security' is runnin' towards me waving a cudgel. So a grab hold of the two transparent sacks, which seem surprisingly light for all that ale, and I leg it back to the time machine, say a little prayer and hit the button.

"And brought back all these cans that somebody else had already emptied." The king gave a hearty laugh. "Better luck next time, uh, is there going to be a next time?"

"Yeah, there is, and soon! Now I'm really curious."

The king made a thoughtful face. "You're getting kind of obsessed with this, aren't you?"

"You bet your sweet bippy I am!" Hershel gave the mound of cans another swift kick, then went back into his cave, returning with a small keg and a couple clay tankards. He poured some ordinary 'wholesale' ale, giving one of the containers to the king, and sat down at the slab that served as a table across from the monarch. "The more I think about this future thing, the more I want to know what it's all about. When I tried on old dead Freddie's trousers, I found some interesting things in the little pouches, there were four of these little bag things sewn into the pants, and there was stuff in each one of them."

"Pouches sewn into his trousers? It sounds like a convenient thing." The king clapped his hands together. "I'll have to mention this to my tailor. Can you show these trousers to him some time?"

"Yeah, sure, highness. So anyway, one of these pouches has a small leather purse thing in it. It was thin and folded over. Inside were more of those paper silver things, but these papers said they were only worth five or ten pounds of silver each. I think there was one or two worth maybe twenty pounds… There was also a big folded up sheet of paper that said it was a driving license, whatever that is, and another hard square thing that said it provided something called 'National Health' for our Freddie. Frederick Sandino is the name on it."

"Most interesting," the king mused, placing his left elbow in his right palm with his other palm stroking his left cheek and a gleam in his eye.

"Yeah, right! And one pouch had a few coins and a ring with what looked like very small keys on it, weird little flat keys. I tell you, this is all too mysterious! He had a handkerchief in another of these pouches, *that* I recognized!"

"Well, you have been busy," the king laughed, taking a long draught of his ale. "I can't wait to hear about your next adventure with this invention of yours."

"I'll tell you, Irv, tonight I think I'm gonna just hit the hay and get some sleep. The future can wait another day or two."

## SIXTEEN

Things were quiet around the Wholesale Kingdom for the next week or so. Merve, the head woodsman, found some nice lumber which he cut down and helped Prince Sol drag to the side of the King's Highway up near the big field of boulders where Sol's buddies, Rowland and Baldric, were digging a shallow ditch. Princess Judith experimented around with making different types of Pizza. She personally liked the very thin crust, like what Hershel the Merlin had brought back from the future, but found many of the king's retainers preferred a thicker, breadier pizza.

Judith also tried putting a variety of items on top of the pies she made. Olives were a big hit, but were pricey as they had to be imported. Shreds of game birds were also good as were small chunks of spiced beef.

Queen Sophie was busy embroidering banners for Prince Sol's roadside attraction. She sewed several that said 'See a real live dragon!' and 'Do you dare? 1 Brass Coin!' She made the flags of a rich golden linen embroidered with bright scarlet thread so they could be easily spotted at a distance.

Hershel the Merlin seemed to be spending a lot of time down at the smithy's shop. King Irv wasn't sure what to make of this but figured it probably had something to do with improving the Merlin's time machine. Maybe Hershel was worried that the tin structure wasn't strong enough to stand up to all the to-ing and fro-ing.

On a fine spring afternoon, after a short shower of rain had passed, Irv noticed that Hershel was back in his cave so he decided to stop by and see how things were going. The sun was shining brightly and there were small fluffy white clouds blowing across the heavens. Yellow daisies were springing up in the grass.

"Hey Hershel! It's been a while," Irv hailed him. "What's new on the time travel scene?"

"Irv, highness! Come on over and pull up a stool," Hershel retorted with a gracious wave. "I haven't been doin' much time travel. I got this new idea I'm working on."

"Another invention," queried the king.

"Well," said the Merlin hesitantly, "I don't know how much invention, but a great idea anyway."

"And what would this idea be?" chuckled the jolly monarch.

"Three words," Hershel answered, putting up a finger to tap the side of his nose, "summer weight armor!"

"What?" the king sputtered in disbelief. "What in the world is summer weight armor?"

"Here," Hershel told him, "let me get you a drink of ale and I'll tell you all about it!" Hershel returned with two tankards of the beverage, settled down on his own stool, and grinned a confident grin. "You know those ale cans from the future? Well, I got to thinkin' about how light they were when there wasn't no ale left in'm. I mean tin is heavy, and steel is even heavier."

King Irv had to agree. He'd worn enough armor suits in his time to attest to the weight of the stuff. He nodded his head.

"So I took that pile of empties we had down to the smithy. He melted them down into bars and he's supposed to be hammering the bars into sheets of metal when he gets a minute." King Irv gave a questioning look and Hershel answered it, "He said my magic metal wasn't a big priority. He had swords to forge and horses to shoe, but he promised he'd work it in somewhere."

"How about we take a stroll down there and see how he's doing with that," Irv suggested. "Maybe his king showing an interest in this new tin will light a fire under the man."

As they entered the smoky hut to the windward side of the castle, a large, broad-shouldered man with a sooty face and hands came forward, spit on his palm, wiped the mitt on his even blacker apron and started to extend it. Then he noticed that it was the king approaching. He quickly withdrew the hand to his side and snapped to attention, shouting, "I'm honored by your presence, your majesty."

"At ease, man," the king grinned. "I just stopped by to admire your fine work. You may call me Irv."

The big man grinned and put his hand out again. "And I'm John."

Irv shook the extended hand and asked, "A smith named John?"

"Smith just sounds so common," the man told him with a self-deprecating look.

King Irv gave a hearty laugh. "Yes, so it is," he admitted. "I'm pleased to finally meet you, uh, John. And by the way, my Merlin brought some mystery metal to you..."

"Ah yes, the ale tins," the smithy said, adopting a serious pose.

"Very interesting stuff, that metal. "I've had a couple cans resting in water all week, and it doesn't seem to rust! It stays shiny. And it's very easy to work with. Here, I've got a sheet of it I hammered out late last night from one of the ale-metal ingots." He dug around behind his forge for half a minute, standing up with a thin, gleaming square.

"Summer is coming soon," Hershel began, looking around the shop nonchalantly. "It must get awfully hot prancing around in your heavy old suit of armor, huh your highness?"

"You got that right, Hershel," the king answered right on queue. "That old armor suit is hotter than the inside of this hut with that fire blazing away. If only someone could make a suit of something like this lighter weight ale-tin…"

"Whoa," John ejaculated. "I think I know what you'se guys is thinkin'. If I could fashion armor from ale-tin…"

"If you could…" echoed the king.

"I'll have to look into that when I get a spare minute," John said with a nod, looking over at the pile of projects on his work bench."

"And how soon…" Hershel started to ask, but John cut him off. "I got to sharpen Sir Broderick's sword and finish that new sword for that other knight that lives over beyond the village, and I got a ton of locks to make along with keys to fit…"

It was King Irv's turn to interrupt. "I am really anxious to try on such a suit. The man that could get me a summer weight suit like we're talking about is liable to be handsomely rewarded. Possibly even a knighthood."

John's head snapped around sporting a lopsided grin. "A knighthood? I think my calendar just got clear, your highness. I'll get right on it!"

# SEVENTEEN

King Irv said goodbye to Hershel outside the smithy. Hershel told the king that he had more work to do, but could maybe meet with Irv later for a drink. The king decided to leg it up the highway to see how Prince Sol's roadside attraction was progressing.

He found his son with his friends, Rowland and Baldric, bracing up their crescent shaped wall of logs with stout cross timbers. Princess Judith and Burny the dragon lay in the tall grass behind the new enclosure. It almost sounded like the huge dragon was purring. Judith stroked his pale tummy scales as she stared into the bright blue sky.

"What ho!" shouted the tall monarch as he approached. Prince Sol turned his head from his work. "Oh, hi pop! What do you think?"

"Very impressive! You boys... Ur *men* have done well in such a short time."

All three of the young lads voiced a 'thank you' to the king, but continued straining against the weight of the heavy timbers. Irv walked around the wall, inspecting the work the young fellows had done. He couldn't help but notice that his son was putting on some real muscle tone. The lad's once skinny limbs now sported well defined biceps and broadening forearms. He smiled to himself and went over to plop his rear into the tall grass beside his daughter.

"Oh daddy, I'm so happy," Princess Judith told him, sitting up and wrapping her two arms around one of his. She rubbed her face against his shoulder. "Sol says he's going to let me sell pizzas to the tourists that come to look at Burny! The punters can watch Burny heat up the rock to cook the pizza and then we'll sell them slices from the pies Burny cooks. Isn't that just a smashing idea! I might even get rich!"

"Honey," her father assured her, "You are rich *already*. I have a wealthy little kingdom here and someday you and your brother will inherit all this! But it's good for you to learn something about work and business. And this pizza thing is a wonderful hobby for you."

"Do you think the people that stop by here will pay another brass coin to buy a pizza? Huh daddy?"

"Well, a brass coin might be a little much. You'll have to wait and see. We'll sit down and figure out just what it costs for you to make a pizza and then we can decide what to charge… And if folks think it's worth that much to sample some new food they've never seen before."

"Oh pop! I just have this feeling that everyone is going to want to try my pizza. And they'll love it too!"

As his heart began to melt once more, King Irv held his daughter close and told her. "I hope you're right. I think you might have something here. I'll say a prayer for you!"

The king looked up to see Prince Sol and his friends had finished bracing their wall and were about to take a break. Baldric produced a small keg of ale from the shade behind their handiwork while Prince Sol dug some clay cups out of his rucksack. "Care for a cup of ale, your highness?" Rowland asked as the boys sat in a semi-circle around the king, the princess and the dragon.

"Oh, just a small one," King Irv replied. Rowland held the cups while Baldric poured. He handed the first cup to King Irv and the second to Princess Judith before seeing to the boys of the work crew.

"I didn't know you liked ale." Irv stated in surprise, watching his young daughter take a sip.

"Well, I prefer that sweet wine, daddy," she giggled. "But ale is what the *boys* drink."

"So why are you and Burny hanging around here anyway," Irv inquired.

"Oh pop," his daughter blushed. "I just like to watch." Then in a whisper, she finished, "those friends of Sol's are getting so *buff!*"

A warning flag went up in the poor kings head, 'ought-oh, my daughter has discovered boys. What will happen next?'

"Ah, sweetheart, don't you have some work to do back at the castle? Don't you think you should be helping your mother embroider some of those banners for your brother?"

"Oh daddy," she laughed. "I'm not going to *do* anything with either of those boys; I just like to watch them work!" She hugged her father again. "Don't you go worrying about me."

Then the young men had finished their ale and were returning to work. Judith went back to stroking her dragon's tummy and Irv decided to go back to the castle for a short nap.

After his nap and a spot of cold roast beef for lunch, the king took a hike down by the Merlin's cave, but he noticed that the time machine was gone and a sign outside the cave proclaimed 'The Merlin is out.'

On awakening the following morning, King Irv dug through his wardrobe to find his old spyglass. When he had it in his hand, he polished both lenses with spit and a linen cloth, and then carried the heavy tube to his chamber window, which stood partially open.

Resting the glass on his window ledge and peering across the meadow, he observed that the Merlin's time machine had returned, so he quickly dressed, grabbed a small loaf of poppy seed challah for breakfast and headed over to talk to his friend.

"So how are things doing in the future?" the king chuckled. "Any more news on what brought my castle down?"

Hershel lifted a couple cans of Mann's Real Ale from under his table, popped the tops and handed one to King Irv. "I managed to make contact there," he told his friend. The king shot Hershel a serious look. "Tell me more," he commanded.

"After I left you and the smithy yesterday," Hershel began, "I started thinking, why not do it now? The time will probably never be any better. So I came back here and got all kitted out in Freddie's clothing. The boots were a bit tight and the pants a bit loose, but I figured 'what the heck.' I adjusted that silly cap thing and screwed it down on my head and full of determination, I got in the old time box and fired her up."

"I noticed that it was gone when I came by yesterday," the king told him.

"Yeah, right. So I bumped myself into the future right in the middle of the afternoon. I strolled around one of the ruins of your castle walls without bein' hit by any flying eggs and, bold as brass, I strutted into the door of the bar in that little cottage there." King Irv nodded that he was listening and Hershel continued.

"So there was, like, three people sittin' in the bar and this really pretty barmaid behind the counter, she had light brown hair worn kinda long and the brightest green eyes I ever laid *my* eyes on! I notice that there's some pump handles behind the bar and one of them says Mann's Strong Ale on it, so I ask this pretty lady if I could have a flagon of the strong ale. She giggles a little, takes this perfectly round glass vessel from a rack behind the bar and pumps it full of ale, setting it in front of me. Then she says, 'I don't think I've seen you in here before, but you've got one of our caps, so you must be a member.' She made a thoughtful face and then she says, 'I know, you must be one of our *London* members that only come up a few times a year!'

"I just sit there and don't say nothing, then one of the other punters at the bar, sounding a little in his cups, already shouts a slurred, 'London! Huh! That accent doesn't sound like London to me! He must be an *American* or something.'

"Then the fellah sitting next to him says, 'And his clothes don't fit so well, yeah, he must be some fool American hick. I don't know why we let *foreigners* onto our course!'

"So I says, 'okay, you found me out. I'm like, what did you call me? An American hick.' The two guys start laughin' really loud.

"Well then that pretty wench behind the bar, she sticks out her hand as she says, 'I'm Josey. Pleased to meet you, uh...'

"Friends call me Hershel,' I tell her and she finishes her sentence with, 'Pleased to meet you, Hershel. Are you staying around here?' Well, I don't know how to answer. I thinks for a minute, then I say, 'No, I'm just passing through.'"

"That was probably a good answer," Irv told him. "In a sense, passing through is just what you were doing."

"Yeah, right," Hershel answered. "So then, one of these guys that had a bit too much to drink? He's complaining about something he calls a golf score. He accuses his buddy of not keepin' an accurate tally, then he turns to me and says, 'so do you play, Hershel?' What am I supposed to answer? I just shake my head and say 'yeah, of course I play.'

"Then he asks me what's my handicap! Now I'm really feelin' confused, do I have some kinda handicap? But his buddy saves me by hollering over to Josie 'lemme shout this fellah a round,' and next thing I know, this pretty girl is setting another full glass of ale in front of me!"

"That was fortuitous," Irv commented. "Although I don't know how you expected to pay for your first drink."

Hershel returned to his story, ignoring the king's comment. "Then the drunk guy says, 'And another round for Clive and me too!' and this Josey lady, she says, 'Oh no, I think you boys have had enough. I don't want to be responsible for you killing someone out there on the highway.' *Killin'* someone, that's just what she said! Well, after that the two drunks, Clive and his pal, they call Josey a bunch of rude names, but they pull out little purses, like that fold-over one I found in Freddie's trousers? And they lay a bunch of those papers on the bar that say they're silver and walk out. I turn to watch them leave out the front window and I see them get into some kind of carriage thing. There's no animals attached; no horses or mules or oxen, but the thing suddenly starts moving and it carries them away down the road!"

"That sounds most mysterious," postulated the king. "Are you sure there were no beasts of burden attached?"

"Hey, Irv, may the Lord strike me down if I'm lyin'!"

"I wasn't questioning your veracity," King Irv apologized. "So what happened next?"

"Well, when Clive and his buddy had gone, I noticed the other guy, who was sittin' way down at the far end, had very dark skin. He looked almost black! This black guy looks over at me and he say, 'Hershel is it? Let me buy you another beer, Hershel.' While I'm thinkin' 'what the hell is a beer?' Josey comes and puts *another* full glass of ale in front of me even though there's still a sip or two left in my last drink.

"So this black man, he comes down and takes the stool next to me, sticks out his hand and introduces himself. 'Rutherford P. Johnston,' the man says. 'I'm a grad student at Oxford.' 'Oxford,' I says, 'you mean down south on the river Thames, where it narrows and people walk their cattle across?' This Rutherford guy laughs. 'Something like that,' he says, then he asks what I do. I start to say I'm a Merlin, but with the words half out of my mouth I think better of it, and I just say, 'oh a bit of this and that.'

"Well, that gets a real big laugh out of this Rutherford guy! 'I've been listening to your accent and observing some of your reactions and mannerisms.' He says it with a really serious face. 'You act like you could be from *old* England, like, a long time ago old

England.' Well, like I want to ask him what is this England place, but I just kinda play along. 'Old England is my field of study,' the black man says. About now I'm gettin' kinda nervous. I tell this Rutherford guy that I think I should be going. Rutherford extends his hand one more time and says, 'I hope I see you around here again. I'd like to talk with you some more. Maybe we could play a round of golf sometime.' I tell him 'Yeah, I'd like that, though I still don't know what this golf thing is everyone is talking about."

"But this Rutherford chap, he just accepted your answer?" asked King Irv.

"Oh yeah," Hershel told the king. "He just ordered himself another ale and sat there staring at a little lump of a smooth, squarish rock or something in his hand that made a beeping noise. I pulled that little purse thing of Freddie's out of the pocket of the trousers I took off him and laid one of those papers on the bar, a paper that said 'ten pounds' on it. Well, Josey, she pushes some buttons on a metal box behind the bar and a little drawer opens. She pulls another paper out and a couple coins and puts them on the bar in front of me. The paper she set before me says 'five pounds' on it and the coins say 'one pound' on each of their faces, but they couldn't have weighed more than a gram each and they certainly didn't look like any silver I'd ever seen. They were pale yellowish in color. Then, feeling my oats, I asked her if it was possible to buy any of those tin containers of Mann's Strong Ale that I could take home with me. She asks me, 'Do you want just a party four, or a case, seeing as you don't live close by.' I said 'how about a case?' Well, Josey went through a door behind the bar and returned with a box made of that same thick paper that the pizza came in. She said, 'That'll be twelve pounds, seven with the tax.' I found a note in that purse thing marked twenty pounds; Josey opened the drawer in that metal box again and gave me another five pound note and more coins. A few more that said one pound on them, but some smaller ones as well. When I got back to the time machine, I opened the lid of that box thingy. There were twelve cans in it!"

"And that's where this ale comes from that we're enjoying right now." Sighed the king, "which by the way, can I have another one?"

"Yeah, sure," replied Hershel reaching under the table into the paper box and popping another top.

"I suspect you'll be going back to the future again soon?" Irv took a swallow from his new can and rested his eyes on his Merlin.

"Well, your highness. That Rutherford guys *has* got my curiosity in high gear after I come back here and think about it for awhile. I need to find out some things, like what is old England and golf… And where is this America place? How did the man's skin get so dark? And how did that carriage move? Could it be something like my little time machine?"

"And I'm sure you'll find all the answers," King Irv chuckled.

# ✦ NINETEEN ✦

With Spring, of course, came tax collection time. King Irv and his knights were quite busy as mid-April approached, but most of his loyal subjects were happy to pay the king his due and within a week. Things were settling back to normal around the realm. King Irv's stores were bursting with grain, fruit and the other items with which his subjects supported Warehouse Castle.

One fine morning shortly thereafter, John the Smith came to the back door of the castle pulling a small hand cart. "I think I got it right, your highness Irv," he shouted from the courtyard and King Irv went down to find out what the man had gotten right. John held up a gleaming suit of armor, so light he could hold it above his head without any assistance. "I made it to the measurement of the original suit my predecessor had fashioned for you."

"It's beautiful!" the king exclaimed, walking slowly around the smith to see the armor from all angles. "Exqui*sité*! I love it. Can I try it on?"

"That is why I brought it to you, my liege," John the Smith smiled at him.

"I keep my regular armor down in the stables," Irv told him. "Let's go down there and I'll slip into this, see how it feels."

John followed the king, towing the armor on his small cart. At the stable door, Irv lifted the suit from the cart and disappeared inside. He emerged moments later fully kitted out, helmet and all.

He'd even taken a moment to strap his best sword on at his side.

"It *is* light weight… And comfortable. It's almost like wearing regular clothes! John, would you mind saddling up my horse for me?"

The smith gave a look of disdain. Smith's were *not* stable boys! But then, his king seemed so pleased with his work, oh, why not.

"Sorry," the king apologized. "I know it's not really your line, but my son is busy building something just up the road. He would normally be here to help me…."

"It's alright, highness," John smiled. "I don't mind just this once."

When John had led the king's mount out into the sunlight, Irv swung himself into the saddle and trotted off, leaving the smith and his cart behind. He rode first to the courtyard, where he shouted up to his queen. "Sophie, Sophie baby, look at me! Check out my new armor!"

The queen stuck her head out the window of her chamber. She pulled a face when she saw her husband in the shining suit. "New armor," she tsked. "What was wrong with the armor you have, already. And just how much is this bit of vanity gonna cost us? Oy, you collect a little tax revenue and you just can't wait to run out and spend it!"

"Sophie, listen to me! This is light weight *summer* armor. The smith made it outta those ale cans Hershel the Merlin brought back from the future! It didn't cost that much to make, and think of the money we could bring into the kingdom if something like this catches on and we're the only people that can provide it!"

The queen shook her head, "I just hope you're right." Then she disappeared back into the window.

Next, Irv rode up the road to where his son was building the roadside attraction. He stood proudly in the saddle as Prince Sol, Princess Judith and their friends stopped their labor to stare at him.

"Wow, pop! How'd you get such a shine on your old fightin' suit?"

"This is new!" Irv shouted at his son. "It's new armor made from those ale cans Hershel found in the future!" As quickly as he said it, he remembered he hadn't told his son that much about the future. Probably had only mentioned the pizza in passing, but Judith saved him further explanation. "I told Sol all about Hershel's time travel," she announced. "And that suit looks great on you, pop, it's so crisp and bright! I think you'll be the envy of all the surrounding kingdoms!"

"I hope so," he told his daughter. "I'm going to look into hiring a couple more apprentice smiths to make a bunch of these and we'll open a shop in the village. Custom fit summer weight armor at *wholesale* prices! Our smithy tailors are standing by!" And with that, he rode off to show Hershel what they had created.

But Hershel's time machine was gone. Pity he couldn't be one of the first to witness what the smith had done with the metal Hershel had, in a sense, discovered. Should he take a gallop into the village to show off to his loyal subjects? He thought better of that. Someone might get the wrong idea and think the king was concerned about an attack or something, so he returned to the stables where he hung his new suit next to the old one, brushed and watered his horse and headed back home for a nap.

## TWENTY

Hershel returned just before dusk. King Irv had been watching for his machine's appearance from his chamber window, too excited to get any real rest. He knew it was close to the dinner hour, but he legged it across the green meadow anyway. Hershel was going to love his new armor!

But when the Merlin emerged from his cave, Hershel looked tired and drawn. "Trouble?" the king greeted him.

"Just a very tense day," Hershel sighed. "But I found out what England is… *We're* England! I mean that's what they call this land around your kingdom in the future. And America? It's another kingdom of sorts across the ocean to the west! And golf? That's some kind of game they play with the sticks and those tough eggs, trying to get the eggs into a rabbit hole or something! Oy, so much information to digest! My head is simply spinning!"

"Hershel," the king bleated sympathetically, "I think you'd better sit down, have an ale or two and tell me this story right from the beginning."

"Yeah, an ale," Hershel parroted with vacant eyes. He ventured back into his cave and came back with four cans still held together by that weird stretchy material, pulled two free and popped the tops. Irv reached across the table and rescued one of the open cans from the Merlin's shaking hand.

"So, you went back to this pub in the future," he prompted.

"Yeah, that's what I did," Hershel spoke softly. "I went back to the Castle Golf Club bar, that's what they call it." His face brightened a little. "I did think to cast a simple spell to make my time machine resemble one of those carriages from the future, a little mild hallucination set upon anyone there that might stare at it. And I figured out how to adjust my space dial just a scoch, so I'd land on that gray, barren field in front of the bar, where the other carriages are parked instead of the grass where all those eggs were flyin'.

"I walked inside. Josey was standin' behind the bar and that black Rutherford guy was sitting way down at the end, where he'd been the other time I was there. I looked around and noticed that we were the only people in the place. Josey caught my eye and told me, "Mondays are always a bit slow." What, I'm thinkin', time moves at different paces on different days in the future? Without my sayin' anything, she sets one of those glass vessels full of ale in front of me and smiles. "So how's your day going?" she asks me. Before I can think of a good answer, Rutherford pats the stool next to him with his hand and says, "Hershel! Good to see that you came back. Come on down here and talk to me!"

"I turned back to Josey and told her my day was okay so far, then I picked up my ale and took it down to the end where Rutherford was parked. The man had a kind of sparkle in his dark brown eyes and he was grinning from ear to ear. 'Hershel, Hershel,' he says and he laughs. 'I'm pretty sure you came here from another place in time... So tell me what England is like back where you traveled from.'

"'What makes you so sure I'm from, ah, some other time?' I ask him and he gives me another chuckle, like, from deep down in his chest. 'Just a feeling,' he says, 'So, am I right?' Then he takes a long drink of ale, watching me over the top of his glass. I'm startin' to break a sweat inside this too tight shirt of Freddie's and the black guy keeps staring at me with that grin. What could I do? I finally cracked. 'Yeah, sure, okay,' I tell him. So I'm from the past, so what! And what is this England, anyway?'

Lookin' toward the ceiling with a wistful grin, he says, 'This is England, right where we're sitting is England. It's a powerful nation, a kingdom on an island in a big ocean. And, though it might have been known as something else way back in history, where you came from was probably England too.' Then he looks me right in the eye and continues, 'If my thinking is correct, you once lived in the castle that left these interesting ruins…'

"'Not *in* the castle…' I said, earning another funny look. '*Near* the castle,' I says. King Irv lived, uh, lives in Warehouse Castle!'

"Rutherford, he gave a laugh so loud and strong, he's spittin' ale all over his shirt and the bar. '*Warehouse* Castle?' he sputters. 'Oh, that's rich!' 'The Wholesale Kingdom has its share of the wealth,' I reply. 'I guess you could call us rich. So tell me more about, uh, England!' 'That's a tall order, he says. 'I'll give you a brief sketch. How's your drink holding up?' I held up my ale, which was getting' kinda low, Rutherford pointed to our, uh glasses, he called them pint glasses, and Josey refilled them."

"So my kingdom will someday be England?" Irv mused.

"A part of England, sire, I'm coming to that. It was a long story. This Rutherford fellow says that the Romans came and organized things, but then they went back to Rome, and a lot of small bands of people got together and established individual monarchies all across the island, and we must have been one of these groups. Lat-

Skoot Larson

er, he tells me, people came from beyond the island. Not Romans, these guys who came were hostile, warlike people, so many of the small kingdoms united together into larger kingdoms. Eventually, we had one very powerful king, a Christian fellow that ended up ruling almost all the island and they began calling it England." The king nodded for Hershel to continue.

"And when the place started getting crowded, some of the people ventured across this ocean of water thing, I guess that's like a really wide sea, in boats. They went to a wilderness place called America. Then these Englanders in America decided to make their own kingdom and they broke off from England. It's more complicated than that, but that's the gist of it."

"And all this happened between now and, ah, when your time machine landed? That's amazing! So how many years did all this take?"

"Well over a thousand years, so Rutherford tells me."

"Wow, that's a lot of years! And to think that some walls of my castle are still standing after all that time! I'm so glad my ancestors didn't skimp on the materials they chose to construct this place." They both laughed at that and raised their cans in a toast to Warehouse Castle.

"So then Rutherford wants to know all about the Wholesale Kingdom, like, how you ruled, how many subjects you had power over, what kind of crops we grew, and then he asked me about the chapel, which is the best preserved part of the ruins. Something he called The Church of England has maintained it over the years and done restoration. 'It ain't no Christian chapel,' I tells him. 'It's, uh, it *was* a Jewish temple!' I expected more laughter, but this real hard look comes over the man's coal black face. 'Seriously!' he barks at me. 'A Jewish temple in the dark ages?' 'And dark ages means?' I ask, and he mumbles something about the enlightenment, then say it isn't important. He takes another long drink of ale, almost drains away half his glass. Then he asks me where in the remains of the chapel could he find proof that it was a temple? 'I'd love to find evidence of Jewish people in old England' he smiles. 'This could turn my ho-hum doctoral thesis around and maybe get me a professorship!' I told him I'd try to think of something."

"And golf?" inquired King Irv. "What is this game called golf all about?"

"That's another long story, Irv. But I think I'm keeping you from your dinner hour. Queen Sophie is headed this way and she don't look happy…"

# 🐉 TWENTY-ONE 🐉

King Irv slept fitfully that night. So much to think about! He wanted to learn every little bit of knowledge he could from the future, but at the same time, he was afraid of what might lay in store. He couldn't wait to talk with Hershel again, but the next morning the Merlin's time machine was gone.

King Irv paced the castle and watched throughout the day, but the time machine didn't return. He began to worry if maybe something had happened to Hershel in his travels. Had the man met the wrong people? Perhaps Freddies' friends that wanted to avenge their buddy's death. What could his friend be doing in this future place that took so long?

The king picked at his supper, leaving the table frequently to peer across the lawn toward Hershel's cave. Queen Sophie was getting fed up with his anxiety. "Irving, can't you sit still for a lousy minute?" she chastised him. "What are you waiting for, anyway? Is news from that mashuga Hershel so important you can't sit down and enjoy supper with your family?" His son and daughter looked away in embarrassment.

The king didn't have an answer. He pushed his hardly touched plate of roast beef and boiled potatoes away, then took himself outside to pace the castle grounds. He watched the sky grow dark and the moon start to rise. The planet Venus was looming large on the horizon. Finally, he caught a glint of light from down by the small hillock where the Merlin had his cave.

King Irv actually ran across the deep spring grasses, ignoring shouts from his wife to 'slow down and be careful!' He reached Hershel's cave even before the man had climbed out of his funny tin machine.

"You were going to tell me about golf," he shouted, half out of breath as he approached. "So where have you been all day?"

"Sorry, your highness," Hershel said looking sheepishly at his king. "Didn't I tell you? I had an early appointment with Rutherford. He said he'd teach me how to play this golf game... And he did!

"So tell me all about it!" Irv barked, still short of breath. "What's it all about."

Hershel looked at his monarch. "Should I open a can of ale for you first, Irv?"

"No! the king shouted. "I mean yes, by all means open a can of ale, get one for yourself..."

"I think I've had enough, already," Hershel slurred at him, reaching into his tin machine and pulling out four bound together cans, popping one which he freed from the stretchy stuff and handed to the king. "After my golf lesson, I put away five or six pints of ale with Rutherford. I almost had trouble figuring out how to get my machine going!"

"So golf," the king threw back at him. "What is this golf?"

Hershel blinked a few times and shook his head rapidly side-to-side as if to clear it. "Well, it's a game, Irv, kind of a complicated game with some ten or so sticks. Each stick has a flat surface attached on one end, and the surface of each of these is tilted a bit different, so when you hit these egg things they fly at different angles into the air."

"Fly at angles into the air? Flat things attached to sticks?" the king responded. "Hershel, this all sounds pretty crazy to me, how much ale did you say you had to drink?"

"The God's truth, Irv, I told you this golf game was crazy. Anyway, you keep whacking these eggs around the countryside. Every so often there's a patch of grass in the center of the pasture that's been shaved down to nothin' and there's a hole in the middle of it marked by a flag. There's like, maybe eighteen of these close-cropped places. When your egg lands on these little circles of short grass, you've got to hit your egg real easy and try and make it roll into the hole."

"And once your egg disappears down the hole?" the king inquired.

"Well," the Merlin hesitated. "I know it sounds crazy, but you pull it outta the hole and whack your egg toward the flag marking the next hole. I'm pretty new at this, so I don't know if I'm telling it all correctly, but I'm gonna go play some more of this golf with that black guy in a few days. I should know a little better after that."

"You do that," Irv told him, feeling a little let down at this explanation. Why would men in their right minds be interested in chasing eggs around the countryside, knocking them into holes, then fetching them out and blasting them toward another such hole? It just didn't make any sense.

On returning to his castle, King Irv found his queen waiting up for him in the parlor. "Can we share a glass of wine?" she asked. "Frankly, I'm a tiny bit worried about you these days. You're so anxious and you're going off in so many crazy directions. I just want my lovable old Irving back here with me!" She smiled and put a hand under his jerkin to stroke the hairs on his chest the way she knew always got him going.

From somewhere unseen, a servant shimmered in carrying a silver salver holding a bottle and two glasses. The retainer poured out wine for each of them. Irv noticed that it was some of the good plonk that was supposed to be Roman which he'd bought at Woburn, over in the next kingdom to the south.

"That will be all, Seth," the queen told the servant. "And please make it known that his highness requires privacy!"

With that, his wife began removing her clothing with a wink. "Come on, Irv, let's relax a little" she purred. "I think you understand about my needs!"

## TWENTY-TWO

For the next few weeks, Hershel was gone more than he was present. King Irv decided it was alright, he'd learn what there was to learn when his Merlin settled down to a more regular routine. In the meantime, he was getting plenty of attention from his queen and he was enjoying watching his children as they prepared their roadside attraction business. John the Smith had hired two apprentices and was setting up an assembly line to produce samples of summer weight armor in different sizes and the landlord of the pub in the village was happy that Prince Sol and his friends seemed to have reformed from their larcenous ways.

Up the highway at the roadside attraction, Judith had asked Prince Sol's buddies to dig a shallow dish in the earth behind their enclosure wall as a dragon pit. She spread Burny's favorite toys, his little stuffed cow and his colorful balls, along the indentation in the ground and began rewarding the beast for spending time in his new bed. Prince Sol completed the dragon lair by constructing a short picket fence to separate it from the space where tourists and the other curious would be herded through. Judith then had them drag one of the broad, flat rocks to the side of the dragon pit, where she could prepare pizza pies with Burny's help while the crowd looked on. They were finally ready to put up the highway banners Queen Sophie had embroidered and wait for customers to arrive.

Upon seeing what a wonderful amusement his children had built, King Irv decided to declare a special festival day on the first of June. They would erect many colorful marquees in the nearby pasture by the field of boulders where they would be celebrating the "Grand Opening" of the dragon viewing sight. Also at the festival King Irv and John the Smith would introduce their new line of summer weight armor to the world.

Travelers along the highway had already begun stopping by, more than happy to part with a brass coin to view what they thought was a dangerous wild thing. And almost everyone that stopped to see Burny was interested in sampling Judith's new bready, cheesy dish.

The king visited the new business almost every day to see how things were going and collect the drawstring pouches of brass that Prince Sol divided up from their takings to be the kingdom's share. On one such day, Deborah, the daughter of Lenny the Vintner and Judith's closest friend, was there by his daughter's side. She had two casks of her father's product and a table bearing a dozen small clay cups.

"Daddy," Princess Judith told him gleefully. "I invited Deborah to bring some wine that folks could sample along with their pizza and everyone loves it! Can we build a small bungalow in our enclosure and make it a wine tasting bar? Lenny will pay Baldric and Rowland to build it. Deborah will tend to the wine bar while I'm making pizza and we'll get even more money from the travelers that come in!"

"You think worldly, well-traveled people will actually give up a coin for that rubbish Lenny makes?" Irv whispered to his daughter in a voice low enough that he hoped Deborah couldn't overhear.

"Oh, daddy," his little girl laughed. "So far everyone that comes in *loves* Lenny's wine! We've gone through most of these two casks already today. It's all how you present it!"

King Irv turned a befuddled face to his daughter. "How you present it? Wine is wine, my dear. How do you *present* this plonk that makes it different or better?"

"May I speak, your highness?" Deborah ventured hesitantly.

Deborah was a tall chubby girl, but a lovely young lady just the same. She had dark eyes that appeared almost black, with light brown curls resting on her proud shoulders and a perpetually fetching grin. She had been Judith's best friend for as long as the king could remember.

"Oh course you may, Lady Deborah! What do you wish to say?"

"Well, your highness, Princess Judith has put clever labels on my father's products…"

"The dark stuff," Judith cut in, "we are calling Dragon's Blood. People can't wait to drink dragon's blood!"

"And Lenny's sweet white wine?" the tall king asked skeptically.

"That's Dragon's Piss," Deborah giggled. "Excuse my language please, your highness. Judith named it."

"The Piss is actually the more popular of the two," Princess Judith added with a positive nod of her head. "Lenny could give us some bottles to sell here as well. If the punters will pay a single brass coin for a taste, I'm thinking we can flog off a full bottle for at least ten coins! Pop, the people are just eating it up… or drinking it up I guess would be more correct. And of course, the kingdom gets its percentage, like with everything else."

King Irv couldn't argue with his daughter's business sense, a roadside attraction with a dragon on display, a pizzeria and a wine shop. It could be almost like a license to coin money! But would the novelty wear off after time? Or would pilgrims walking the King's Highway spread the word and bring even more business?

The king smiled to himself. Only time would tell. In the meantime, he made a mental note to have one of his knights ask around the merchants in the village and see if any of them would be willing to spare a coin or two to put up a handbill on the attraction's enclosure wall advertising those merchant's wares and directing the tourists to their places of commerce in the village. I could maybe do a trade out with the landlord of the pub, he thought. I'll give his advertisement a prime location on the wall in order to cover my bar tab. But I will still tip the serving wenches, he grinned to himself. It's always worth a coin or two to see their happy smiling faces, not to mention the cleavage they each exposed.

#  TWENTY-THREE

The June Festival arrived before King Irv knew it. Prince Sol's friends had completed Deborah's wine bar with the help of Merve the woodsman and the roadside attraction was an amazing sight to see. Many of the village merchants had purchased advertisements on the attraction's outer wall and were already reporting an increase in out-of-town business.

The colorful tents were spread around the pasture adjacent to the roadside attraction, along with a raised dais for Queen Sophie and King Irv at the field's edge, where they could judge contests of courage held between the kingdom's knights and other loyal subjects. Irv's men had set up an open area for jousting and an archery range, as well as a wide arena for mock battles among his knights with swords and other personal weapons. The king's administrators had a long list of potential contestants waiting to take part in all the events of the afternoon against his noble men.

The landlord of the village pub had rented a marquee of his own where he opened keg after keg of golden ale for the strolling crowd at two coins a cup. In the wings, John the Smith waited with young men prepared to display summer weight armor in a sort of manly fashion show.

God seemed to be bestowing his blessings on the event with a bright blue, cloudless sky and mild temperatures. Gentle breezes stirred the surrounding forests with just enough wind to cool the summer day and insure everyone's comfort. King Irv couldn't have asked for more clement weather.

The king had seen little of Hershel the Merlin over the weeks leading up to the festival. When he *had* run into the man, their conversations were brief and meaningless. Hershel always seemed to be in a hurry and his mind was away somewhere, worrying about his golf game and his new found friends in the future. King Irv was too wrapped up in the affairs of state and his festival to worry about it.

There proved to be a lot of interest in the new, lightweight armor suits after John the Smith held his introductory ceremony and fashion show, although no one actually stepped up with the silver to buy one. Like anything new, Irv figured, it would take time before someone would be the first to shell out the high price the smith was asking. But once the first suit was sold and seen out in the world, he felt confident that more orders would follow. Who wouldn't want to lighten their burden as they marched forth into battle?

Princess Judith and her dragon had a long queue of villagers waiting to sample their pizza. Much to the crowd's consternation, they ran out of both cheese and bread dough long before the sun set on the festivities. The locals weren't fooled by Lenny's clever labeling of Dragon's Piss or Blood, but they consumed enormous amounts of his local wine just the same. The longest queues were at the latrines, just through the trees in the W. C. Fields!

King Irv gave a speech about love and brotherhood as things were winding down and the shadows growing longer. Queen Sophie waved and blew kisses to the homeward bound crowds from their blue and white bunting covered pedestal. The king was anxious to get with his tax people and see just how much this little event had put into the kingdom's coffers. There was surely a handsome profit after the participating merchants paid their percentages of gleaned revenue and when all the expenses of the festival had been deducted.

It was only three days later that John came to King Irv with the good news that he was custom fitting light weight suits for four different knights from two of the neighboring kingdoms. The regent of the Wholesale Kingdom's closest neighboring patch, a Christian fellow named Bertram, was footing the bill for his trio of noblemen. The man couldn't wait to see how smart his noble fellows would look stepping out in the gleaming new metal coverings. The fourth customer was a sort of free-lance dragon fighter who called himself The Hot Knight.

John said he had measured all four and promised delivery of their armor within a fortnight, with a wink to his helpers that promised a big bonus if they aided him in keeping his word.

# TWENTY-FOUR

Hershel did finally turn up on the king's doorstep one afternoon a few weeks later. The man kept bouncing from one foot to the other foot, anxiety oozing from his pores. He did not seem happy.

"Hershel, my friend!" King Irv greeted him, arms outstretched in welcome. "Haven't had a chance to talk in ages! Come in, I'll get you a drink."

The Merlin continued his worried dance. "Oh, yeah, a drink would be good..."

"You appear upset, my friend," the king smiled. "Is something the matter?"

"Ah, yeah, funny you should ask, highness. Something is *very* the matter!" He blinked a few times, took a deep breath and barked, "That black guy, Rutherford? He wants to come here and meet you. Like from the future... *Meet* with you! I ain't got a clue what to do... Or what to tell him! What the hell I'm I gonna do?"

King Irv swept an arm toward the castle's back door. "First I think you'd better come in and have a seat. I'll have one of my servants bring us each a large ale and then we can discuss it. Relax! I don't think that a visit from this man would be the end of the world."

"You wouldn't mind talking to this guy? Or putting him up as a guest?" The words rushed forth from Hershel's mouth. "I mean he ain't from around here, well I mean his *is* from around here but not in our time...."

"Oh come on, Hershel. It might just be fun," the king chuckled. "Haven't you enjoyed talking with this fellow? He's teaching you about this golf game, maybe he can teach me too! And he's your friend, right?"

"Well, yeah," the Merlin mused. "But is our world here ready for this kinda surprise, maybe even shock? And how do we tell people about time travel? I'm not sure I want to admit that I've been traveling through time. Do you understand that?"

"It's not like we're going to be parading this man through the village," laughed the jolly monarch as one of his retainers shimmered into the room with two tankards on a silver tray. The two men paused, plucked their drinks from the servant's tray and sampled the potent ale. "I think we can keep this all here in the castle and not even say too much to my staff. Your friend will simply be another visiting dignitary."

"If you say so, Irv." Hershel thought for a minute. "So how do we explain his strange clothing and the weird way he talks?"

"Hershel, Hershel, it is a king's prerogative to entertain whomever he likes from wherever. We are not required to answer difficult questions if I chose that they shouldn't be answered." The tall monarch took a long draught of ale and thought for a minute. "We'll just say that this man, uh..."

"Rutherford," Hershel supplied.

"Yes, we'll say this man Rutherford is simply an emissary from the land of England! And we won't be lying, will we?" Irv gave his Merlin a conspiratorial wink.

"Well, yeah," Hershel replied with a grin. "You got that right... Okay, Rutherford of England it is!"

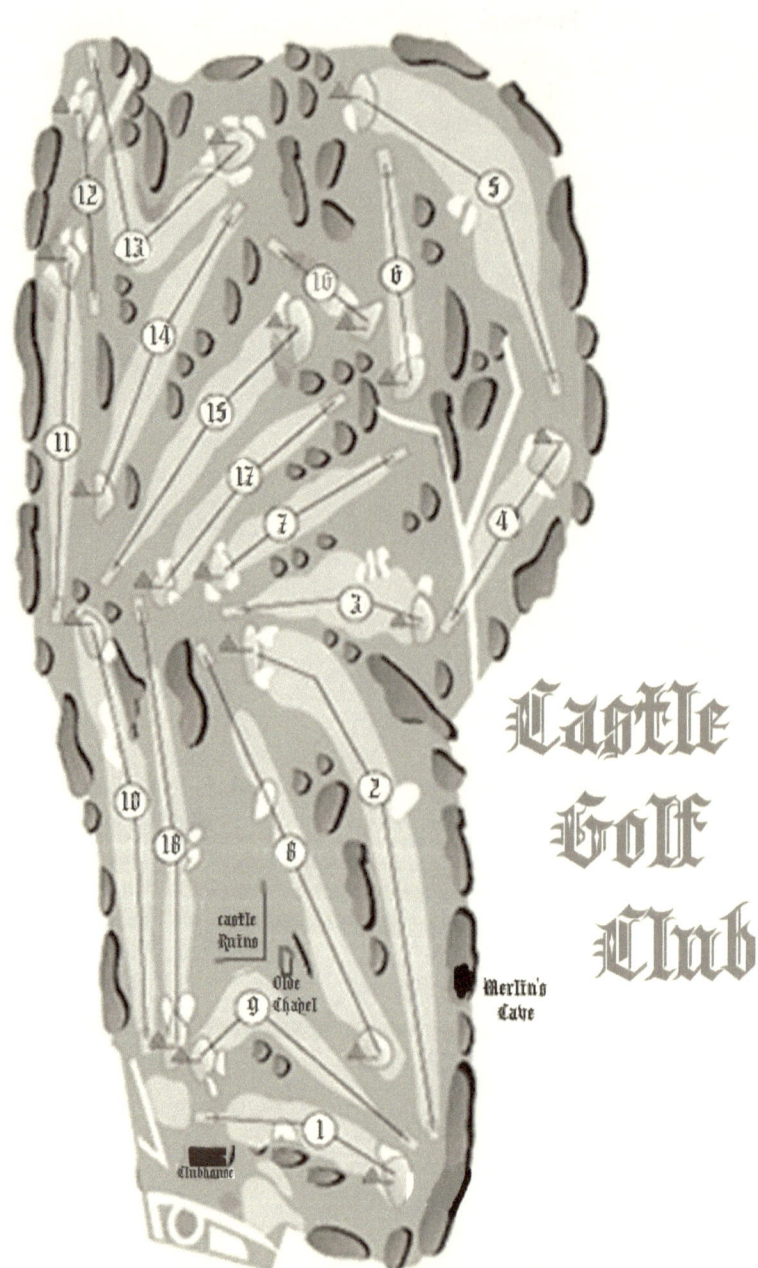

Castle Golf Club

# Part II

# The Arrival of Rutherford

# 🐉 TWENTY-FIVE 🐉

It was mid-afternoon on an overcast spring morning when Hershel's time machine brought the large dark fellow from the future to Warehouse Castle. An anxious King Irv had been pacing the battlements most of the day. He had his spy glass in a pouch at his side, and had been fiddling with it off and on, watching for his Merlin's return.

When the machine began to materialize, King Irv hurried down the stone staircase in the south tower, two steps at a time. It wasn't everyday that a king met someone from the future! He hoped this man, Rutherford, would enjoy the banquet and entertainment that Queen Sophie had planned for the evening. Irv had taken his wife into his confidence about Hershel's time travel and their expected guest. At first his lady thought he was making a joke. "And just how much drink have you had this fine day, Husband?" she asked him.

"Okay, I know you might think I'm totally mashuga, but I'm serious! Hershel has been traveling through time…."

"What do you mean 'traveling through time? How does one travel through time, Irving?"

"He invented something that bumps him into tomorrow, through the next day and the next year. I don't know how to explain it. He just *travels* through time!" The king shook his head in frustration. Seeing his consternation, Queen Sophie parked her hip on the arm of his throne and took his hand, aiming a serious gaze into the king's eyes.

"You're right, it sounds crazy, Irv. Such a thing I've never heard of. So tell me about this traveling across time."

King Irv related everything Hershel had told him. He explained about pizza, and ale in tin containers. "Ach, I wondered where Judith got that idea," she smiled. Irv continued his tale. He tried to explain about the game called golf. And he summed up his lecture with the news that the very dark skinned man would soon be arriving from some future day; that this schvartz was to be their special guest.

Sophie was still quite confused by Irv's strange tale, but she was a dutiful queen and she set right to work planning a menu and delegating tasks to their servants. She asked her secretary and head of staff, a man called Jeevestein, to line up some amusements for the banquet.

King Irv crossed the meadow at a quick step, only slowing as he made his final approach. Hershel and his dusky guest were busy unloading packages from the time machine. Irv recognized the cartons that contain ale tins, four of them! And what looked to be a large satchel, but the leather bag that was unloaded next was quite foreign to his eyes. It had some kind of weapons poking out of the opening at its top.

"Golf clubs," Hershel laughed, following the king's eyes. "These are the golf club things I've been telling you about." Then the other man turned around. "And this is my pal Rutherford," Hershel added, indicating the large black man that was setting his baggage on the ground. "Rutherford, this is my liege, King Irving Benjamin Abrahamson, We just call him Irv."

Irv shook hands with the jovial, grinning black man. Rutherford had a powerful handshake. He also had kind, inquisitive eyes and his smile was full of warmth. "It's such a pleasure to finally meet you, your highness," he said to Irv in a mellow baritone. "I've been hearin' so much about you and this place."

"I've been hearing about you too," the tall king replied nervously. He wasn't sure just what to say next. Hershel saved him.

"Hey Irv, what say you summon a servant or two to help us haul this ale down to the banquet hall where it can be stored in your cool pantry. And while they're at it, maybe someone can take Rutherford's bag to his room. You might show Rutherford to his chambers so he can freshen up from our thousand-year ride." Both Hershel and his dark guest got a good laugh out of that. King Irv shuffled his feet nervously then said, "Oh, well, yes, of course. Please, Mr. Rutherford, do walk over to my castle with me. We have a nice suite of rooms waiting for you. My men will fetch all these packages to the hall straight away."

Once Rutherford had checked out his rather Spartan quarters and unpacked, he descended the grand staircase to find Irv and Hershel sipping tins of ale in the main hall. The king snapped his fingers and one of the castle's retinue materialized from behind the stairs with another tin of ale on a silver salver. Rutherford took the proffered can and the tall king popped up to take his elbow and guide him to a very comfortable divan opposite where he and Hershel were parked.

The men made small talk for the remainder of the afternoon. King Irv promised Rutherford that he would personally show him around the grounds the next day, but this evening he thought they should just kick back and get to know each other better.

After discussing the weather, how often it seemed to rain around here, both in the present and the future, and how sports differed from now 'til then, Rutherford cleared his throat. "Your highness," He said, "I'd like to get serious for just a moment. As Hersh might have mentioned, I'm an Oxford scholar in my time. That's a kind of very advanced student in school. In my time there is so much to learn that many of us attend schools we call universities for much of our lives."

"I've heard of schools," Irv offered. "In my neighboring king- doms, which are mostly Christian, the church runs public schools. Here in Wholesale Kingdom, our children learn trades from their parents. They go to Torah study at the temple on the Sabbath, but that's about it, so I don't know anything about advanced schools or anything called a university."

Rutherford chuckled at that. "Understandable, your high- ness…"

"Please, call me Irv," the king prompted.

"Yeah, okay Irv. Anyway, one of the things we study is the past. Like where we came from and what happened in the world before we were born."

"Kinda like Torah study," the king mused.

"Yeah, kinda, but a lot more intense, I guess you could say. Like in my case, I'm researching the early post Roman history of this island we live on. I'm trying to learn all I can about past times, like right here where you and your kingdom are living. And that's why I wanted to meet you and talk to you. We have an expression, 'pick your brain' meaning to discuss thing together until I understand all about what you're thinkin'."

"Pick my brains? And you can do this without killing me and opening my head," Irv asked in all seriousness.

Hershel and Rutherford both laughed at that. "Nobody has to get hurt, highness," Hershel grinned, poking a thumb at Rutherford. "This guy has been pickin' my brains since I first met him and I'm still alive, healthy and full of oats!"

"Hmmm," sighed the king, "We'll have to see about that one. But right now, one of my family members seems to be signaling to me. I think it may be time to eat. Let me guide you to our banquet hall."

## TWENTY-SIX

I t was a most magnificent feast, with four courses and a pudding for dessert. They began with trays of raw vegetables, followed by a rich, creamy broccoli soup, then small roasted game birds, and finally braised beef as the **pièce de résistance**. The afters were a tasty caramelized custard that Princess Judith boasted was her specialty. And of course the red wine flowed. Not the local vintage, but more of those so-called Roman bottles King Irv had bought for his wife.

When the dishes had been cleared and the ladies left for their own little gossip session, Irv had his retainers bring cigars and a heavy distilled liquor he only brought out on special occasions. He asked the man that brought their after dinner smokes if his queen had indeed hired suitable entertainment.

As if on cue, Morrie the Court Jester appeared far down the hall, then disappeared again behind thick curtains that lined the hallway. Morrie was a stellar entertainer. He could play the lute, sing, dance, juggle colorful wooden balls and he was also a very funny man.

Morrie bashfully poked his head out from behind the curtains halfway down toward the kitchens. He pulled his head back out of sight, and then jumped fully out, spreading his hands to his sides and shouting, "ta-dah!" The jester then came forward to take center stage wiggling his eyebrows up and down and continued.

"I just got back from Londres. Oy, the traffic, nose to tail all the way! I had to put a bumper sticker on my cart that said, 'keep back, my horse has diarrhea,' heh, heh, heh!"

"Hey, Morrie, tell us that one about senior night at the theater," the Merlin said with a mischievous glint in his eye.

"You sure you want that story? The queen said she didn't think it was very amusing."

"Ah, go on, Morrie! The queen is upstairs putting the kids to bed," giggled the king.

"Well… okay then." The jester focused serious peepers on his audience. "See there was this guy, Ish the Hypnotist. He was real good at what he did, so they booked him for senior night over at the theater, you know, something fun for the old folks. When all the sexagenarians had taken a seat, Ish says 'I'm here to put you into a deep trance, so deep a spell that it will knock out each and every person in the audience.' Well, the excitement was almost electric as Ishy withdrew a lovely glass pendant from his waistcoat. 'I want you all to keep your eye on this crystal pendant,' he told them. 'It's a very special piece that's been in my family for generations.' Then he began to swing the crystal gently back and forth while quietly chanting, 'Watch the pendant, watch the pendant.' The crowd became mesmerized as the crystal swayed back and forth, the candle light sparkling off its polished surface. Dozens of pairs of eyes followed the swaying piece of jewelry until suddenly it slipped from Ishy's fingers and fell to the floor, breaking into a hundred pieces. '**Shit**!' cried Ishy."

"That's funny?" questioned Rutherford.

"Hey, already," Morrie replied straight-faced, "it took three days to clean up the theater and get rid of the smell..." At this point King Irv and the Merlin both lost it, laughing so hard they spilled their brandy down their tunics.

"Ishy was never invited back," Morrie finished with a broad grin.

"So where did you find this guy?" Rutherford asked when their laughter had died down. Morrie jumped right in chuckling, "Hey, I can't help it, I was raised in Vaudeville!"

"Vaudeville? Come on," the scholar laughed. "Vaudeville isn't over a thousand years old! And it came from America anyway."

"Well, I don't know how old it is." Irv mused thoughtfully. "And I don't know about 'from America,' but Old Mel says King Vaude already had the place just to the east of us when we moved here." Morrie nodded quickly in the affirmative.

"Wait just a darn minute! Someone better explain this to me. Morrie, you say you're an entertainer and you grew up in Vaudeville, so what is this Vaudeville *you're* talking about?"

"It's about seventeen miles east," King Irv put in after taking a conservative sip of his remaining brandy, "Just outside Vaude Castle. They've got a great theater there. Oy, can those people act! They do Greek, Roman and they got a well-endowed damsel there dresses up like a dragon then takes her costume off one scale at a time until she's in just her long underwear! It's fantastic!" He swilled some more brandy then wiped his mouth with the back of his hand. "Hey Morrie," he shouted, "How about you play us a little song!"

# ⚔TWENTY-SEVEN⚔

I n the morning, over a large breakfast of kidneys, eggs and fried tomatoes, Rutherford asked Irv, "Who is this Mel the Old that your court jester Morrie mentioned last night? Morrie said Mel told him some history about the Vaudeville place. Does this Mel know a lot about the past of the area?"

"Oh, you must mean Mel of the brooks, yeah, he a wise old guy, or an old wise guy. He lives in an abandoned grain mill." Irv said after swallowing a large mouthful of grub. "Old Mel is always talking about what he calls 'the good old days,' so he probably could share some stories with you, like, what you call history."

"Any chance of me meeting this Mel guy? I think he might be a big help to me." Rutherford had put down his fork and turned a solemn face to King Irv. "I've got a feeling this man might be the key to what I'm seeking,"

"Mel?" smiled the king. "I mean he *does* have some knowledge, but oy, can he talk! He'll talk your ear off with his stories. Have you got that kind of time? I mean I was hoping you could show me some things about this golf game."

"We'll have time to try and play some golf," Rutherford replied, losing his grave expression. "I'm on summer holiday from school back home, so it's not like I have to be rushing off in a day or two."

"Well then, Mel is easy enough to find, I mean if you really want to subjugate yourself to that. Hershel can take you to the river that runs through here. Just head north at the water and follow the stream as it flows. When you come to a series of brooks, cast your eyes across the stream and look for the old mill. It's easy to recognize, it's almost falling down."

"Thanks, Irv," Rutherford told him sincerely. "I think I'll head down there right away, as soon as we finish this wonderful meal which, by the way, isn't that different from what people are eating for breakfast to this day. I mean in my time, in the future."

"Hey," Irv chuckled, "if it ain't broke, why fix it? But maybe you should have a word with Rabbi Weiss first. If anyone knows the history of this place, it should be the Rabbi. He's our spiritual teacher! The temple is right on your way to the stream and he could maybe save you a lot of time!"

Rutherford found the temple easily enough. It was the building known as the chapel in modern times. He entered cautiously and called, "Is anyone home?"

"Is anyone home?" came a sarcastic reply. "Does this look like a home to you? Oy, this isn't a home, this is a place of worship, so mind your manners."

"I'm looking for the Rabbi," Rutherford stated. "Rabbi Weiss."

"Well, you found him. That would be me, so who are you? I don't recall any schvartses in this neighborhood."

"Excuse me, sir." How did one address a Rabbi? Rutherford had no idea. He'd never encountered a real live Rabbi before. He silently cursed himself for living such a shallow life.

"Your Excellency, your worship?" he tried.

"Wait just a cotton pickin' minute! Hold onto your yarmulké! Ach, but I see you're not wearing a yarmulké! So what do you want with my temple? You're not one of these Christian rabble-rousers?"

Rutherford turned a thousand candle-power smile on the short, balding man. "Whatever should I call you…?"

"Try Ibraham," the short man inserted.

"Ibraham," Rutherford continued, "I know it sounds far-fetched, but I'm here from the future…"

"Yes," the Rabbi mused in a hearty voice. "Such a thing could be expected," he said ethereally.

"Ah," Rutherford cleared his throat. "Ah, I'm not some sort of religious sign or something… I'm just a historian looking for facts, information about our history. I mean the history of this land."

"I've heard there might be such a thing," the teacher replied pensively. "You're a schvartz! According to the old traditions, this Christian savior, Jesus, was also a very dark skinned man. I don't believe in coincidence. But at the same time, I don't know how I can help you. Are you gonna claim to be another savior?"

"No, I'm not even that religious. Can you tell me about the history of this kingdom?" the dark man asked.

"Ach," the Rabbi replied. "The Torah, I can tell you all about it, but the lives of men? That's not my field. Perhaps you should speak with Mel of the brooks. This man Mel, he knows about the past affairs of our people. He's the oldest man in the kingdom. He kinda keeps track of things like where we came from. He might be able to help you. He lives in a little falling down dab and waddle hut by the river that used to be a grain mill."

"Mel's in the mill?"

"Isn't that what I said? Just go knock on his door and tell him the Rabbi sent you to interview him. He loves to talk about the old times! Get him started about history, you won't be able to shut him up, believe me,"

Rutherford said goodbye to Rabbi Weiss and excused himself from the temple. He strolled along the eastern pasture to the river, then turned north where the cry of mating ducks led him to the first small brook. He walked on. There was a noisy waterfall from this small body of water to the next larger pond. Just beyond the tumbling liquid he spied the crumbling ruin of the old mill. Farther downstream, he could also see a much newer structure where men were depositing sacks of grain for grinding.

Rutherford came to a stone bridge just before the falls. He crossed the bridge, approached the older building, and gave a timid rap on the oaken door.

The door was opened by a bent, emaciated and wizened figure with an unruly afro of frizzy white hair and a bulbous nose like a bloated bagel.

"You must be Mel the Wise," Rutherford greeted him. My name is Rutherford."

"Mel, that's me, but I'm not so sure about the wise part anymore," the old fellow laughed. "You, Rutherford did you say you call yourself? You're not from around here."

"Well, no," Rutherford answered. "I'm a scholar and I'm studying the history of England to write my thesis. I'm working on my Doctorate at Oxford…"

"England, you say? Doctorate? Oxford? I know nothing of these things! I think maybe you came to the wrong guy." The man started to close the door in the black scholar's face.

"Wait," said Rutherford, a little louder than he intended, placing his size twelve basketball shoe in the door jamb. "I truly believe you can help me! I want to learn how a kingdom of Jewish people came to be here in a primarily Christian land. I want to learn all about your history!"

"Christians and heathens... History I know, but they send a schvartz to learn our history? What are you, from Ethiopia? I remember hearing they got some pretty smart people in Ethiopia, at least back in the day."

"No, I'm not Ethiopian; I'm British, from England..."

"There's that England place again. What is this England?"

Rutherford hesitated to gather his thoughts. It would sound extremely fanciful to this old guy, but what the heck; in for a penny, in for a pound. "This is England, right here, we're standing in England, er, at least this land *will* be England one day."

"It will be one day? What, are you some conspiracy nut planning to overthrow the king? Huh?"

"No, no, nothing like that, please just listen for a minute." Rutherford took a deep breath before continuing. "I, uh, well, I come from the *future* to learn about your past. I know it might sound crazy to you..."

"Crazy, smazy," the old man smiled. "One hundred years I've lived. I seen some crazy shit, I've *heard* some crazy shit. You've got an honest face." Old Mel took Rutherford's face in his hands, breathed deeply and thought for a minute. Then he patted the dark man's cheek and leaned back against the door motioning Rutherford to enter. "Come, sit down, my friend. Can I get you a glass of ale? No one in this kingdom seems to care a fig about what happened in the past or how we got here, so I might as well trust this knowledge with you. I think I've only stayed alive this long in hopes that maybe that lazy prince or someone would take an interest and write down some of what I know …"

Mel the Wise pulled a clay jug from a niche in the wall along with two tall hand-blown glasses. He poured them each a generous taste and motioned Rutherford to a stool at a small wooden table. Mel took a seat of his own, sipped at the golden liquid and smiled an expectant smile at his new friend.

Rutherford reached into his coat pocket for a spiral-bound pad to take notes. He fished some more until he found the short stub of a golf pencil. "So tell me, Mel, how did your people come to this land and establish a kingdom here?

# 🐉 TWENTY-EIGHT 🐉

"It was a simple matter, really," Mel began with a faraway look in his eye. "Our folks were among the first Jews to immigrate to Rome, after all that Christian business began. We were a small colony, maybe a half-a-dozen families with us. Well, we weren't well received, I can tell you. The more the Christians prospered, the more difficult they made it for us. Finally the emperor at the time, Theodosius the Great I think they called him, he came up with a solution to our kind in order to secure the popular support of all these loud mouthed Christians."

"The first final solution," Rutherford mused.

"First, I don't know, but that's what they called this pogrom when the soldiers came to round us all up, a final solution!" Mel frowned and shook his head. "We thought we were all gonna wake up dead, never mind that God was looking out for us."

"Wow!" Rutherford exclaimed. "And you have this all written down somewhere?"

Mel tapped two fingers against his forehead. "Up here I have it, it's all up here!"

"So what happened? Obviously they didn't kill all of you."

"They didn't kill *any* of us," Mel tsked. "We were a quiet people, not trouble makers. We kept to ourselves. We didn't get drunk on wine and start fights or stab people. We worked hard and we lived a simple life, a *family* life. For however much they might have blamed us for murdering their so-called savior, the local gendar-merie had some respect for us and they passed the word to the soldiers at the local garrison."

Rutherford was writing furiously, licking his index finger and flipping pages in his notebook as he wrote.

"There was a ship setting sail for some distant colony they called Londres that night..."

"That would be ancient London, the capital of modern day England!" Rutherford barked excitedly.

"Ach, there you go with that England schtick again! So you want I should continue the story?"

Rutherford nodded silently, his eyes wide.

"So they brought us up to this Londres place, oy what a grimy, smelly city, a real backwater after living in Rome. And the rain? Always, it was either foggy or raining. Our people worked hard in spite of it was so cold that a person could perish and when we saved most of what we could earn and as fast as we could, we blew that dirty popsicle stand. We bought ox carts and a few animals and we headed north into what the locals called the wilderness. That was, what, six, seven generations ago?"

"That would be maybe a hundred and fifty years?" Rutherford was calculating in his mind as he spoke.

"A little longer than that, I think," Mel mused.

"And Theodosius I, I think he's the one that they called 'the Great,' so that would mean you were exiled toward the end of the fourth century! That would make the year around 650 or 660 AD right now."

"Listen, Mr. Rutherford, you're talking way beyond me, okay? Let's keep it simple and I'll finish my story!" Mel closed his eyes and reverently said, "Always, my own sweet papa, God rest his soul, he used to say remember a kiss; keep it simple, stupid!"

"Okay, we'll keep it simple." Rutherford nodded his head rapidly up and down. "So you traveled north into the wilderness…"

"Yes!" Mel replied loudly, "that's just what we did. We encountered a lot of stuffed shirt, self-proclaimed Lords and Earls that told us to just keep moving, keep moving. Then one morning we saw a lot of smoke on the horizon!"

"Smoke?" Rutherford queried. "Like from a bunch of village chimneys or more like big fire?"

"Oy, it was a big fire, all right. Village chimneys was all that was left all around a big field of boulders! Ach, and the smell of death? So many burned bodies! Women, children, old, young! We couldn't find a living soul, I tell you. I mean, I wasn't there, but this is what my papa and his papa before him all said."

"Amazing! An entire village wiped out? But by whom… and why?"

"Listen, back then, we didn't ask questions. We buried the dead, we built walls and we rebuilt the burned buildings. We went back to the Torah and we re-read the story of Jericho over and over. Whose Jericho had this been? And we waited, scared shitless that whoever had burned the first village to the ground would return to wipe us out as well!"

Rutherford's pencil was flying over the pages. He had resorted to a sort of shorthand he had invented to take notes in his undergraduate classes.

"But they didn't come back! Out of fear, we dug a moat, built the castle you see over there, and our little temple just outside the castle walls. We would welcome the occasional traveler that happened by, always trying to be good hosts."

"You didn't have any neighbors? Or trading partners?" Rutherford interrupted.

"No mention is made of that, so I couldn't honestly say. I just know we had travelers. Pilgrims, I think they were, bound for some holy place or other. By the time anyone asked, we had been living here long enough that everyone assumed we *owned* the place. My papa's papa *christened* this, if you'll pardon the expression, to be the Wholesale Kingdom. Oy, what a salesman he was! Somehow, he figured out that people, *all* people, are always looking for a bargain!"

"And the temple?" Rutherford asked. "Is there any documentation of any of this that might be buried in the temple?"

"Well," Mel said with a burning look, "perhaps I shouldn't be saying anything to a non-religious foreigner and a schvartza besides… But who else is taking any interest? You're from the future you say? Maybe it would be for the best…"

Mel sat silent for a long while, empty eyes lost in deep thought or prayer. "Alright, God, alright," he finally muttered. "Come with me, come, Mr. Rutherford. Come with me, we'll walk through the temple and I'll show you where you might look. But only in the future, you must promise me. Only *way* in the future!"

# 🐉 TWENTY-NINE 🐉

That evening, Rutherford returned to the castle wearing a big smile. The plan forming in his head was beyond his wildest belief. If he could find the hidden cache Mel the Wise had told him about under the chapel floor, if it was still there? Find it, get it vetted and verified, and then get this all into his doctoral thesis, he could easily get a professorship, live a charmed academic life and have plenty of time to play golf and drink ale. He was so happy that he'd met Hershel and had the opportunity to travel through time, although he prayed that not a word of this time travel wheeze would ever reach the ears of his Oxford colleagues.

Rutherford asked one of the king's serving wenches to fetch him a can of ale from the pantry, then he settled into a couch in the main hall to read over the notes he'd taken at Mel's mill. So much amazing information, he could hardly wait to get back to the computer in his three room flat in Aylesbury.

He ticked off points that he might be able to further research in support of all he'd learned this wonderful day, marking lines with asterisks and putting his thoughts in longer notes on the book's back pages. His concentration was broken by the sound of footsteps from the hallway.

"Wendy, the downstairs maid, said I might find you here," came the voice of King Irv from behind the staircase. "So I gather you found our Mel of the mill? Was he helpful, did you learn anything useful?" The king walked into the room and parked his regal frame on another divan opposite Rutherford.

"Your Mel was an immense help!" Rutherford beamed, looking up to meet the king's eyes. "He is just a fount of useful information," the black man smiled holding up his four-by-five spiral-bound pad. "What I learned from Mel might just shake down the halls of academia!"

"I'm not sure just what all that means," chuckled the tall monarch, "but I'm glad we could be of some small help to you."

"No, your highness, a *big* help!" Rutherford spread his arms wide, holding his notes out to one side and his stubby pencil to the other. "A huge help, like I never could have believed!"

Wendy the maid shimmered into the hall at this point with a tankard of ale for the king. When Irv had his drink, the young girl turned to Rutherford. "And is sir's ale holding up well?" she queried. The dark scholar lowered his head, peered into the tiny opening in his ale can, then tested the weight of the tin with his hand and told the girl, "I'm probably about ready for another if it's no trouble."

"Serving is no trouble, kind sir. It's my calling." The young lady smiled and curtsied.

"I think I'd like to sample some of the local brew," Rutherford told her, tipping his head toward King Irv's tankard. "When in Rome…"

"Are we in Rome now?" Wendy asked with a befuddled look.

"Ah, just an expression, dear girl," the dark man laughed.

With a cloud of confusion still tinting her pretty face, Wendy departed to fetch another ale for what she considered to be 'this strange black fellow.'

"I learned so much today," Rutherford told Irv. "So tomorrow I'll try to fill you in a little on the game of golf. The clubs I brought with me? They're Hershel's sticks, actually. I brought a couple extra putters in the bag so we would each have one. Putting is such an important part of the game."

Then catching the monarch's perplexed look, he added. "I guess I'm getting a little ahead of myself here. You'll learn all about putters and putting tomorrow. The putter is the smallest golf club and most useful for the final act of knocking your ball into the hole. And I figured your blacksmith could study the golf clubs I brought for Hershel and then maybe he could figure out how to forge another set for you, your highness. He could make some with longer shafts, as your highness is taller than Hersh."

"That would be appreciated," King Irv told him. "I can't wait to see this, uh, putter and learn how it is used. In the meantime, we've a less formal dinner planned for tonight. My daughter, Judith, is preparing the meal for us. She is preparing a specially seasoned cut of beef that she calls 'pastrami.' She serves it on loaves of bread cut in half with a sauce she conjures up from the roots of the horseradish plant.

"Yeah, I know pastrami," Rutherford told Irv. "It's still popular in my time. You say your Princess daughter invented the stuff?"

#  THIRTY

King Irv went to his window upon awakening to check the weather. It was a bright, sunny day with just a hint of breeze. A perfect day to learn how to play golf! Down in the south pasture, he noticed that Hershel was overseeing a dozen or so of his vassals that appeared to be crawling on their bellies in the newly mown grass. It must be something to do with this golf thing he told himself, but for the life of him, he couldn't figure out what it might mean.

The king dressed hurriedly and ran outside to ask Hershel what they were doing. He grabbed an onion bagel as he passed through the kitchen and hot-footed it out through the meadow to where his workers were assembled. On arriving, he noted that each of his retainers was armed with a small pair of sheers. Hershel sat in their midst with a trowel, digging in the dirt.

"Hershel my friend, what goes on here?"

The Merlin looked up, shading his eyes with his left hand. "Oh, hey your highness, we were just preparing the green for you."

"Green? Green what?" the befuddled king replied.

"The *golf* green, you big nut, er, your highness." Hershel gave him a funny look and turned back to the place where he was scooping out earth. The Merlin picked up the bottom of an ale can someone had cut in half, placed it in the ground and then started packing soil all around it to hold its opening level with the lawn.

Tapping his foot nervously, the tall monarch looked on in silence for a minute, then posed another question. "I don't get it... But then I'm just the ruler of this small land. You're preparing a golf green with a dozen of my vassals on their hands and knees wielding scissors while you dig in the dirt to bury an ale can. What am I missing here?"

Hershel turned his face up to his king, then he put down his spade and stood. He dusted the dirt from the knees of his funny checked futuristic trousers and spoke. "Irv, you don't know a lot about golf yet, okay? Once you start learning the game, it will all make sense, I assure you. See, you've got to have one of these circles of very short grass at the end of every golf hole..."

"A hole at the end of every hole," Irv pondered. "You're talking riddles. Is this something like holding up two mirrors so you can see yourself getting smaller and smaller in the glass until you're not there?"

At this, Hershel burst into laughter. "Nothing so complicated as that, highness. Each 'hole,' that's what we call the area from the start to finish of each leg of the game, begins at the place you call the tee-off and ends with a circle of very short grass with a hole in the middle to putt your ball into..."

"You mean to *put* your ball into it?" questioned Irv.

"Eh, well, yeah but you put the ball there with your *putter*, so technically, you *putt* it in." Hershel could see from King Irv's face that the man wasn't getting this. All around them, the retainers were trimming the lawn in an ever increasing circle. Hershel walked to one edge and paced off the distance to the other side. "Almost there, guys," he shouted to the workers, "Just another half a meter." Then to Irv he said, "Let me demonstrate. Hershel walked to the edge of the ring of trimmed grass and picked up one of those sticks the king had seen in Rutherford's open leather bag. "This is a putter." He handed the club to his king.

Irv looked the stick over, top to bottom passing the shaft along his grip as he went. Glancing at the club's head, he asked, "Does this putter have magic powers? Can it keep wild beasts away?"

"What," barked the Merlin. "What are you talking about?"

"It says 'Tiger Woods' on the flat thing on this club. Will this stick ward off wild tigers in the woods?"

"Oy, Irv! It isn't magic. That's some guys *name*, a golf player that Rutherford says is the best player ever. This guy is *named* Tiger Woods and Hershel bought these clubs because they're just like the ones this Tiger Woods guy uses, get it? Here, let me get out a ball and show you." Hershel began digging in his pockets for a golf ball, but behind him he could hear his king's frustrated sighing.

He turned back to Irv. "Highness? I think maybe we'd better wait until Rutherford can sit down with you and explain how the game works. I don't seem to be very good at telling you how it's supposed to be. How about we go get some breakfast and wait for the man?"

Irv glanced at the untouched bagel in his hand, then back to his Merlin. "Good idea, Hershel. This bagel would be much better with a smear of cream cheese on it."

After polishing off a full plate of bagels with cheese, Irv and Hershel walked back outside to find Rutherford seated around an outdoor table chatting with Rabbi Weiss and Friar Agnello, the

Catholic priest that served two of the neighboring kingdoms.

"Top of the morning to you, your highness. Golf class is just about to begin!"

"Good morning, Rutherford, Rabbi, Friar." Irv tipped his head to each man in turn. "So Rutherford, what brings these men of God to our little gathering? Has something spiritual gone amiss on this fine day?"

The dark skinned man chuckled. "Golf," he answered, "is more fun if you're playing with other people, competing with other golfers. I took the liberty of inviting the good Rabbi and he, in turn, invited his friend Giovanni. If they learn this game as well, you can always get up a foursome."

"A foursome?" parroted the monarch.

"I think we're getting ahead of ourselves again," Hershel put in. "We're gonna have to do this slowly and methodically. His highness, King Irv, is already pretty confused just watching me get the green ready. How about you do a little lecture thing on how the game is played before we start trying to learn the rules?"

## THIRTY-ONE

T he black scholar stood professorially at the head of the small table. "Let's start with the basics," Rutherford began. "Golf is a game played outdoors on a large plot of land called a 'golf course.' A golf course has either nine or eighteen holes."

His audience nodded their understanding. Rutherford continued. "We keep score by counting how many times you must hit your, uh, golf ball before you land it in the hole. The person with the lowest score is the winner."

"The *lowest* score?" asked Friar Agnello, "Not the highest?"

"The lowest," Rutherford assured them. "You try to sink your ball into each hole with as few strokes, hits with your club that is, as possible. Each hole has a suggested number of these strokes that it should take to get your ball in the hole. This number is called 'par.' If you can sink your ball in par you stand a good chance of winning. If you sink it with one stroke fewer, it's called a 'birdie.' Each birdie enhances your chances of making a winning score. Has everyone got that?" Three heads nodded in unison while Hershel just smirked.

The dark skinned scholar went on to explain about each club, the wooden-headed drivers for distance, the many irons and the putter. He described the angle of each club's head and what it meant for giving the ball loft and arc. When he was sure everyone understood about the various golf clubs, Rutherford produced some folded squares of paper from his rear pants pocket and passed them around. "This is called a scorecard," he lectured. The cards had Castle Golf Club, Wholeton, England printed in forest green on the front and a small but detailed map on the back. In the center of the map, where a letter X marked something called the 'clubhouse' and the 'first tee,' the south and east facing walls of the castle could be seen as green lines. "When you open your scorecard, Rutherford continued, you'll see a kind of grid that lists each of the eighteen holes and what par is for each hole. The grid is where each player pencils in his score for that hole and there's a square at the bottom to add up the number of strokes for each hole and get your final score. You then compare the final scores among each player to determine the winner."

"Ah, could you repeat all that one more time?" questioned Rabbi Weiss. "I got hung up looking at the map on the back of my card. Tiny letters there have my temple labeled as 'Chapel.' Could this be correct?"

"I'll explain that to you later, Rabbi," King Irv told him. "Let's concentrate on how to add the score numbers for now."

Rutherford went on and on, talking about fairways, sand traps, putting too much slice or hook on the ball and many other topics. At some point, Princess Judith brought a large tray filled with cold cuts of meat, cheeses, fruits, slices of bread and small cakes which she set out for the golf neophytes. Wendy, the downstairs maid, brought ale from time to time, but the men were too engrossed in Rutherford's teachings to eat or drink.

The sun had passed its zenith and was starting to descend when the dark skinned man announced, "I think it's time for us to try putting some of this knowledge to work. If you'll follow me down to our new putting green, we're going to have a little putting practice."

They walked a determined pace to the close-cropped patch of meadow grass where Irv had earlier watched his staff trimming the turf with their shears. Someone had attached a red triangular banner to a switch of willow and poked it through the ale can that Hershel had buried there so it was sticking straight up, waving in the gentle breeze. The flag bore a bright blue number 1.

"This is our putting green," Rutherford announced. "When King Irv finishes constructing your golf course, this will be the green for the first hole."

"And how will our good king know how and where to build this golf course beyond this first green?" questioned the Rabbi.

"We're gonna build it just like the little map on the rear of the scorecard," Hershel answered in a confident voice. "I've played the course that's on the map there, so I can be like a consultant to the king's men while they're getting this all together. I'll show' em just where everything goes."

"And is the kingdom *paying* you as a consultant?" questioned the good Rabbi.

"No, eh, nothing like that," Hershel assured with just a hint of intimidation in his voice. "I just like playin' golf. I want to have this local course for us to play on, so I don't have to keep goin' to the, uh, never mind. I just want to be of service, you might say."

Friar Agnello laughed at this. "Greed rears-a its ugly head. This greed is a sin, is it not? So what-a if the man makes a sou or two if the work he delivers is-a good?"

"Ah, let's not get into that right now," cautioned King Irv. "We're here to learn how to play this game. If we decide it might be fun, then let me worry about constructing a course for us to play on."

Rutherford passed out the putters that he had brought with him. He unzipped a long pouch on the side of the golf bag Hershel had carried out to the green, withdrew a handful of golf balls and dropped them at the edge of the manicured grass. The dark man then gripped one of the putters with both hands, put both his knees and feet close together, leaned forward and did something he called 'addressing the ball.' He gave the ball a soft tap and all the assembled men watched it roll over the short turf to where it hooked the edge of the hole under the flag. The ball spiraled once around the edge of the ale tin turned cup and dropped in. "See how easy that is?" barked Hershel. "Anyone else care to try it?"

Friar Agnello folded his hands in front of his coarse brown robe and gazed around challenging the others to go first. "I'm the king here," Irv chuckled. "I should be the first to set a good example."

Rutherford handed Irv a putter club with a longer shaft than the others. "Because you're a bit taller," he told the monarch. King Irv addressed one of the golf balls at the edge of the green. He mimicked Rutherford's stance very nicely, then tapped the ball with the longer club. Unfortunately, the king's tap was just a tad stronger then the black man's had been. The ball followed a similar trajectory toward the flag, but as it nicked the corner of the hole, it veered off to the right and continued on until it hit the longer blades of grass at the green's edge. "Damn," the king shouted earning stern looks from Rabbi and Friar alike. "You did very well, highness," Hershel told him. "You just need some practice."

"A lot of practice," the king answered, swinging the putter to and fro in front of himself.

# 🐉 THIRTY-TWO 🐉

By the time Rutherford had to go back to school all his local pupils had become reasonably good putters. The king's men had also finished putting up something Rutherford called a 'driving range' where they could practice hitting balls straight and far with the other clubs in their golf bag. When they would practice on the range, they would hit balls into the field until they ran out of the special missiles. Then they would stop and wait as the castle's grounds staff scurried around the field collecting all the small eggs so they could begin again.

King Irv had his knights go to the local pub to recruit villagers that could work on laying out his royal golf course. The king offered a fair wage and had no trouble putting together a sizable crew of gardeners, laborers and overseers. He watched with satisfaction as the royal course started taking shape.

One late evening as he strolled by his children's roadside attraction he found his son, Prince Sol, at one of the tables in the wine and pizza area with coins spread out in small stacks of ten each. The young prince had a scroll of parchment on which he was tallying up the take and doing sums for the task of dividing up the total; fifty percent for the kingdom, thirty for himself and his workers, and twenty for Judith. He also had coins collected from the winery on another part of the surface ready to be incorporated into the kingdom's share.

Without looking up from his work, Prince Sol said, "They've made me the 'manager' now,"

"Manager?" his father inquired. "What does that mean?"

"It means I 'manage' everything that goes on here. I coordinate all the activity around this place, assign tasks and see that everything is running smoothly. Of course that's what I've been doing since day one anyway, but it's nice to be recognized. I'm also responsible for our marketing plan."

"And just what is a marketing plan?"

"It's a scheme I've devised to make things appear more attractive than what they really are, like when Deborah started calling her father's wine Dragon Blood? Last week I started a rumor that pizza is an exotic dish from Rome and that it's all the rage on the continent. We've also started handing out coupons that the punters can redeem in village shops for a discounted price on goods. When the merchants receive one of our coupons, they know that we've referred the customer to them and they give us a small percentage of the sale. Many of these shoppers, they know, will come back again and spend more or refer their friends. Things are going extremely well, dad. And never mind 'wholesale,' people are willing to pay big bucks for this crazy new dish cooked by dragon fire! Judith has doubled the price to two coins and doubled the tariff for a whole pie as well. No one has made a single complaint. And the more pizza they consume, the more wine they want to purchase from Deborah, which, of course, puts more coinage into the royal coffers.

"For my next move, I'm thinking of hiring some of those wandering minstrels. I'm going to compose a few catchy jingles about our pizza and Deborah's wine and pay these guys a few coins to sing our little ditties between their own more serious works to put our names in the back of the minds of the villagers who hear them."

"And you think this will bring in more business?"

"Trust me, dad. If I can write catchy enough tunes, the citizenry will be singing about us without even realizing what they're doing."

"You've done very well, my son," King Irv told him. "I can truly sense my royal blood coursing through your veins!"

"Thanks, dad! You know I just want to make you and mum proud. And thank you for booting me off my lazy duff! I can't believe that a year ago I simply wanted to get drunk, stare into the sky and do as little as possible! This working for the betterment of the kingdom has given my life true meaning. I will now be proud to follow in your royal footsteps, father."

King Irv didn't know what to say. He daren't answer for the tears that were so close to the surface. Instead of speaking, he folded his son into his arms for a stout hug. When he'd gained control of his emotions, he simply uttered, "Thank you, son. You could never know just how proud of you I am… and your sister too. Maybe if you get a day off sometime, I can teach you this new golf game and we can play golf together."

"I'd like that." Prince Sol told his father. "I'd be honored to learn about golf and to play a game with you!"

Irv found his queen in the dining hall gnawing on a cold chicken leg. "I was getting hungry, but I wasn't sure what you wanted to do about supper," she told him.

"That cold chicken looks good to me," he replied. "How about I open a bottle of wine for us?"

"That would be nice," Sophie smiled up at him.

King Irv rummaged around in the pantry, returning with a bottle and two clay cups. "We're down to just two bottles of this good stuff," he told his wife. "Remind me to make a trip south and secure us another case or two."

"You might not have to make that ride," Queen Sophie told him. "Judith says she's doing so well with the pizza dishes she's offering, she wants to embellish the pies with some more varied toppings. Sol met with a salesman that imports food things from the continent and he says they plan to order Italian olives, some big peppery sausages and some small fish they call anchovies. Why not add a few cases of Roman wine to their order? Sol could pay for it out of the Kingdom's share, couldn't he?"

"I'm sure he could," Irv mused. "But I'd rather give him the coinage to pay for our wine. The roadside attraction is *his* business and I don't want to be seen as taking more than the kingdom's fair share from him. When is he planning to be put in his order?"

"He told me the man is traveling north to solicit more orders tomorrow. He said the salesman needs enough orders to pay for hiring a small boat for the trip across the channel and on to Rome. The man should be coming back through here in a week on his way to Londres. That's when Sol will finalize his order."

"Perfect!" sighed King Irv. "Can you think of anything else you might like from Rome? I'd very much like to get some little thing to please you, wife!"

Queen Sophie giggled. "Oh Irv, I wouldn't know what to ask for. We have so much right here in our little kingdom…"

Irv found a wheel of good cheese in the pantry, which he brought out and placed on the table. "Nothing is too good for my baby!" he told his queen. "How about when we finish the chicken, we take the wine and cheese up to my bedchamber?"

# 🐉 THIRTY-THREE 🐉

The continental merchant told Prince Sol that his order of olives, sausage, anchovies and wine would be delivered within two months, as long as the seas were favorable. King Irv decided he should probably make a ride out and purchase at least a half dozen bottles of the so-called Roman wine from their neighbors in the next kingdom on the Londres road. He and his queen were going through the stuff at a good clip and he was thoroughly enjoying the benefits.

Life was good! Two holes of the golf course had been completed and one of John the Smith's helpers had already fashioned King Irv a set of the iron golf clubs with longer shafts for his taller stature. The smith had told Hershel that he had no idea how to manufacture the wooden driver clubs but one of his apprentices, who had a shiksa mother and had attended Friar Agnello's school in the next kingdom, had taken woodworking courses. The young man set to the task of shaping the driver's heads and grafting them onto the metal shafts the smith produced.

Just when it seemed nothing could ever go wrong in the Wholesale Kingdom, Irv was delivered a summons to a Council of Kings at the court of his neighbor to the west, King Bertram. No explanation was given, but King Irv had a bad feeling about this turn of events. He assembled an entourage of his best knights, his Merlin, and Rabbi Weiss to accompany him.

King Bertram's main hall was filled to overflowing with knights and commoners alike. There appeared to be standing room only and the gathered crowd was extremely restless. Vendors at the entrances were doing a land office business selling ale and cold meats. As King Irv and his retinue entered, some of the folks even booed and cat-called!

Approaching the table in the front of the hall, at which four other area monarchs were seated Irv stated in a loud, proud and clear voice. "I'm King Irv of the Wholesale Kingdom and I am here in answer to your assembled Majesties' summons."

"And do you know why you have been invited here?" King Bertram called down from the elevated stage.

"I only know that my humble presence has been requested," Irv answered. There came more hoots and calling from the assembly in the main hall. He thought he caught the words 'murderer' and 'heathen' amidst their raised voices.

King Bertram held up his hand to silence the crowd. It took almost a full minute, but at last there was quiet.

"Four of my knights went into battle wearing your creation, 'summer weight armor,' I believe it's called. To a man they were slaughtered."

"Slaughtered?" came King Irv's humble whisper.

"Yes. Swords sliced through their armor like hound's teeth through rotten flesh! So what does King Irving have to say for himself?"

"I don't know what to say, sir. I don't know how such a thing could happen."

"You *did* test this new metal in battle, did you not? What were your results? What is this light and shiny metal anyway?"

"Test? Did we test it? I don't know how to answer, good sir…"

"I'll assume that means there were no trials to determine the durability of this armor. So is this armor something that your Merlin conjured up. If so we'll have this Merlin's head!"

"No, please! Mercy my brothers. We did not test this metal. We simply assumed that it is metal and *metal* is strong. Honestly, we meant no harm to your good knights."

"Ah, but harm did come to them! Also, we have another petition before this court. An independent knight who was aligned with no kingdom but works at slaying dragons for all of us and called himself The Hot Knight, his widow tells us that he stood before a dragon and was literally cooked in his 'summer weight' armor. The metal of his suit actually *melted* into globs upon his frying flesh!"

At this point in the proceedings, Friar Agnello from the village church jumped up and shouted "Deviltry, witchcraft! It's-a Satan showing his-a hand! These are *not-a* Christian people we are dealing with, sire."

King Irv was shattered! He had always thought of the good father as a friend to him and his people. He requested a few moments to confer with Hershel and the rest of his troops. Rabbi Weiss was shaking his head and looked like he was almost ready to disown his errant king.

Finally, King Irv and his Merlin approached the bench. "Your assembled highnesses," he began. "I stand guilty as accused of creating faulty armor, but I had no idea that such armor was not as advertised. My Merlin, Hershel, and I beg the mercy of this court. My Merlin tells me he found this metal in a field. He assumed that it was sent to us by the Gods. Apparently, he was wrong, but how could we know this.

"In restitution for our obvious sins, I would hereby like to offer to the widows and families of these brave fallen knights one gold bar each, and if one of these knights had no family, may his gold bar go to the crown of his kingdom."

Bertram's Queen, face flushed bright red, leapt up from her throne near the assembled rulers to object, "How can you put a price on a human life! This is a totally unacceptable offer, my good king!"

But the wife of one of the slain knights interrupted the proceedings from her seat in the front row. "A real, gold bar? Not just a few gold coins?" she shouted, "I've never even *seen* a real gold bar before. I think we should accept!" She turned seeking support from the other widows seated around her.

The other two wives rapidly agreed with their fellow partner in grief.

A loud mumble erupted from the crowd. 'Gold' seemed to be the topic leading to a loud cheer. Bertram's Queen was over-ruled.

The other assembled kings called a sidebar conference to discuss this turn of events and exited the hall into a smaller chamber. When they returned, King Bertram took the center stage once more.

It is our mutual and irrevocable decision," he announced, "That our good and honorable neighbor, King Irving, and his respected Merlin, Hershel, are to be pardoned as long as the gold they have promised is delivered by sunset two days hence. And an extra gold bar will be required as well for Friar Agnello and the Church of Rome, ah, to forestall any headway Satan might gain through this faulty armor. Also, it is hereby proclaimed that any further suits of summer weight armor produced must bear a 'consumer protection' label painted on the side in bold lettering that proclaims 'This armor is not intended for battle! It is for ceremonial wear only! The wearing of this suit in battle can cause injury, dismemberment or death!' So be it!"

"And just what is this term ceremonial?" came a boisterous voice from the assembly. "You know," King Vaude, also a member of the panel told them. "Like for parades or Holy days."

King Irv and his entourage saddled up to ride home. Hershel turned his horse to face the others and said, "That was a close call and this kinda tension make me really thirsty. How about we stop at the nearest public house for some ale? I'm so relieved by the favorable verdict that I'll shout the first round." The others loudly rumbled agreement and the horses were steered toward the Bertram Arms Pub just beyond the castle off the high street.

As they dismounted behind the tavern, Irv heard a pitiful mewling that seemed to come from under the ground before them. He shushed the others, turned an ear towards the ground and listened, creeping forward in small steps. After traveling about a yard, he spotted a rusted grate set into the dirt where rainwater could drain down to the River Cherwell. Poking through the grate was a tiny ginger-colored paw. "Hershel," he called, "come give me a hand."

The two men wrestled the grating away and a miniscule ball of orange fur came bounding out, leaping onto King Irv's shoulders and disappearing down the neck of his tunic. A loud purr emanated from the king's clothing as the tiny fuzz ball snuggled in. "I think you've made a new friend," Hershel grinned at his liege.

"I believe I have!" Irv smiled back. "We have rescued a small gaolbird!"

"A gaolbird?" the Rabbi asked from his saddle.

"Yes," answered the king. "That's just what this poor soul is. And so I shall name him just that, Gaolbird."

The group all dismounted and headed into the bar, where they were seated at a large corner table. Gaolbird ventured forth from the sleeve of King Irv's coat and turned to face him with a loud, hungry 'meow.'

A rotund man in an apron with a thick red brush mustache came to take their drink orders. He glanced downward to the tabletop and the small fur package. "Oh, has another of those pests found his way in here? Those pesky felines multiply faster than the rats they're supposed to be keeping from my establishment. Never mind, majesty, I'll take him out and drown him." The man reached out toward Gaolbird, who raised his back, unfurled tiny claws and gave a loud hiss.

"You'll do no such thing," Irv shouted loud enough to turn most heads around the pub in his direction. In a quieter voice he continued, "I'll get this fellow out of your hair by taking him home to my own kingdom, *after* you've served us all pints of your best bitter ale."

The mustachioed man shuffled from one foot to the other. "I

dislike cats." He proclaimed. "But it is your highnesses preroga-tive if you wish to remove this creature from my property. I'll fetch your ales for you then," the man sneered.

"And while you're about it," Irv shouted at the landlord's back. "Could you be so kind as to bring a saucer of milk as well?" The landlord shrugged his shoulders without turning around and continued on behind the bar. "Impertinent lout," Hershel said to the man's departing back. "He is a rather rude sort of bloke," Rabbi Weiss added.

Friar Agnello entered the bar, looking all around, finally spot-ting King Irv's entourage and hurrying their way. "Sire! My good King Irv!" he shouted. "I'm so glad I caught-a up to you. I owe-a you at least an explanation if not-a an apology as well."

"Well," the monarch stammered. "I was quite hurt by your words back at Bertie's castle…"

"Irv, you are my friend-a! How-a you doing? You know its-a nothing personal."

"We're okay, Giovanni," Irv said with a face that plainly said they were not. "You were just doing your job."

The Catholic priest's eyes were pleading for mercy from his old buddy. "You know I gotta, how you say, look like-a the big-a noise-a in front of my people, huh?"

The king offered a thin smile. "No offense taken, Giovanni. Why don't you stop by for a glass of wine at the castle sometime? Sophie'd love to see you."

"Hokay, but none-a that-a swill your man-a Lenny cooks up, huh?" "Giovanni Dominic, would I serve that to my friend?" Irv was starting to warm to the old Italian once again. "I've got a bottle or two of a hearty red I bought down the road by Woburn Abby. It's supposed to come all the way from Rome."

Their conversation was interrupted by a buxom barmaid balancing a tray before her. The girl placed the edge of her burden on the table and began shuffling tankards of ale to all the king's men. At the end of the tray, she brought out a dish of milk for Gaolbird and a glass of red wine for the padre.

"King Bertie has a wine maker here in Berten-on-Cherwell?" Irv asked Friar Agnello.

"Ah, no," the good friar told him. "I gotta this guy brings me a cask or two from-a Roma sometimes."

"And you keep a cask here at this public house?"

"No, Kelsy, the guy that-a owns this place, he's-a the man procures it for-a me."

"Kelsy the cat killer," Hershel tossed in.

"What-a you say?" asked Friar Agnello. Irv and Hershel told the good friar all about finding the helpless kitten in the drain, and the landlord's reaction to their find, over countless refills of grog. As they spoke, Gaolbird ventured across the board to rub against Agnello's coarse robes and settled in with a loud purr.

From beyond the windows came the voice of a wandering minstrel wailing, "You've never known of heaven divine, until you've partaken of Dragon Blood Wine, and never you'll taste something so delish, as the roadside attraction's rich pizza dish."

# 🐉 THIRTY -FOUR 🐉

King Irv arrived back at Warehouse castle a bit late as well as a little tipsy that evening. He parked himself on a divan in the main hall and found a ball of string to entertain his new found pal. Princess Judith, seeing the light in the main room, ventured forth to check on her father.

"Judith, my darling young girl," Irv slurred on seeing her, waving his hands about. "You must come over here and meet my new friend!"

"A new friend, daddy? I don't see anyone there with you." Judith gave her father a look that questioned his sanity.

"'E's right here," the king giggled, producing the small orange ball from the buttoned V of his tunic.

"Oh, daddy! Is that a kitten? Oh, he's just beautiful!" His daughter rushed over and parked herself next to her father on the settee.

"Bird? Meet Judith," King Irv told the tiny presence. "Judith, this is Bird."

"A *cat* named Bird? Daddy, you're squiffy." She laughed.

"No, really!" Irv reiterated. "His full name is Gaolbird as we freed him from a small prison, but I'm just gonna call him Bird!"

As Judith took a seat the small ginger kitten jumped to her lap, climbed up her sweater and gave her a stout lick across her face.

"Oh, pop, I just love him! Bird, do you want to stay here with us?"

The furry orange ball answered with a resounding "Me*yeow!*"

Later that night, when Queen Sophie went up to check on her husband, she found the king flat on his back across his broad bed, still fully dressed and the loudly purring kitten fast asleep on the middle of his broad chest.

"So you go to a special meeting with the other kings and you come home with a baby cat," Queen Sophie questioned the next morning over a breakfast of boiled eggs with little toast soldiers. At the mention of a cat, Bird's small head poked out from the neck of Irv's dressing gown. "Was this meeting something about animal rescue? Did they have some complaint about our Burny?"

Irv shook his still foggy head. "No, not animals," he managed, "armor, summer armor."

"And for your summer armor they awarded you a kitten?"

King Irv pressed his balled fists against his temples to try and clear his thinking, but the headache from the previous day's ale wouldn't let up.

"I'm sorry, my darling queen," he began, "things are still a bit foggy. From the conference, we stopped at the Bertram Arms for a drink. The man that owned the place was extremely rude! He wanted to drown this poor little fellow," Irv indicated the kitten that was now pulling at one of the buttons on his garment. "The man tried to hurry us out of his establishment, but as he had been so rude, we decided to stay there just to needle him. I guess we closed the place for him and then, when he brought the bill, we told him that he would get no satisfaction because of the manner in which he treated us. He summoned King Bertram's sheriff, but when the lawman recognized us, he was hesitant to say too much. And when we told the sheriff about the unacceptable behavior we had endured, the sheriff told us to just go, but cautioned us not to come back to the Bertram Arms again. He told us King Bertram would put the landlord in his place and then settle with him."

"So, husband," Sophie scolded, "you got yourself eighty-sixed from the pub in our neighboring kingdom with just a tiny ginger maugy to show for it." She shook her head. "Irv, sometimes I just don't understand you!"

Later, when his hangover had calmed some, Irv opened a bottle of wine and told his queen all about the meeting while stroking the bright ginger fur ball in his lap, about the knights who had died wearing his smith's light weight armor, and the settlement that he had made with his neighbors.

"I plan to put a stop to John the Smith's making this summer armor," he told Queen Sophie. "I think John can be much more helpful making golf clubs instead. If this game catches on, there'll be a big demand for golf clubs."

Queen Sophie rolled her eyes back in her head in frustration, but Irv was so focused on the new game he was learning that he never noticed. He was building the world's first golf course! Never mind that he was stealing the thunder of some future true inventor, he would be remembered as the man that gave England the game of golf! "So what do we think of that, Bird?" he asked the kitten batting at the brass buttons of his tunic.

# ☙ THIRTY-FIVE ❧

The last time they'd seen Rutherford he had said he was going back to the future to work on something he called his 'thesis.' Nothing had been heard from the man now in many months. Fall had come, followed by a mild winter and the start of a very wet spring. And then one damp March morning Hershel's machine returned bearing the broadly smiling black man. Rutherford was even more effusive than his usual self. He'd brought back a modern frock for Queen Sophie, a floppy red sun hat for Princess Judith, something he called a knit golf shirt for Irv, that had Castle Golf Club embroidered across the left breast, and two more cases of Mann's Strong Ale. Lastly, Hershel unloaded a box that made a clinking sound, which the scholar said was to be a surprise.

Hershel was in the same chuffed up mood later when they met with Irv. "Rutherford has some good news, I mean *Doctor* Rutherford!" the Merlin told his king. "But he wants to wait and announce it at dinner. Do you think you could organize a banquet on such short notice?"

For once, King Irv was at a total loss for words. He cast his eyes down to the now much larger ginger puss weaving his way around his ankles. Princess Judith, who'd been listening from a distance, bounded forward shouting, "Yes, of course. We'll have a special big feast tonight. I'll organize it myself if mummy isn't up to it!"

Over a supper of braised beef and stewed cabbage, Rutherford began his tale. "As I may have mentioned before, I have long been a student of history and I've recently been working on an advanced degree. Last year, when I came to visit, I was sent to speak with one of your subjects, King Irv, a man you called Mel the Old or sometimes Mel of the brooks."

Queen Sophie bowed her head. "Poor old Mel, God rest him. The man died shortly after your last visit. He told Rabbi Weiss that his mission in life had been fulfilled after he spoke with you, good sir."

"I'm genuinely sorry to hear that, I mean about his death," Rutherford answered, bowing his own head. There followed a few moments of silence as they all looked introspectively into their own memories of the late wise man. Bird the cat saw an opportunity here and tried to jump up on the table, but as the maugy had grown, they had banished him from the dinner table when he had begun snatching more than his small share of their meals. Judith grabbed him by his haunches to stay the cat's progress. Over Bird's angry protests, the dark-skinned scholar resumed his recitation.

"In my time away from Warehouse Castle, I've been writing a paper, something we learned men call a 'thesis.' Thanks to all of you, and especially our late friend Mel, I had new information about the history of your time in our land, which in the future is known as England.

"In the time where I live, it had been forgotten that Jewish settlers took a part in this island's ancient story. Mel told me how your tribe came here from Rome and of the trials you endured to establish a kingdom of your own here. But best of all, Mel was able to point out to me where I might find physical evidence, proof of his story."

"You found proof that we were here?" King Irv questioned. "Wasn't the walls of my castle that are still standing in your time proof enough?"

Rutherford answered with a chuckle. "Oh sure, the walls still stood, but there was no way to prove who might have built them. They were just a crumbling part of some very old building. And to make matters more confusing, the Christians of my future time, calling themselves the Church of England, have laid claim to your temple, positing that it is one of *their* old Christian places of worship. The first king anyone recognizes was a fellow a few generations after your time, someone called Æthelred the Unready."

"The unready?" questioned Princess Judith. "If the man was unready, why did they let him be king?"

"That's a good question, m'lady," The dark scholar said bowing to the young princess with his brightest smile. "But Æthelred the Unready isn't a part of the history I recounted in my paper. My thesis is entitled "The History of the Jewish Tribe In Post Roman England," and recounts your own story from the time when your ancestors departed Rome until your small kingdom was swallowed up by a larger alliance of royal kingdoms."

King Irv was on his feet with an angry look. "We were swallowed up by other kingdoms? Where did you hear that? That can't be true!"

Bird took advantage of the tension between the king and the scholar to leap up and steal a slice of beef from his master's plate. He dragged his prize to a corner where he tore at the meat contentedly.

Rutherford shrugged his shoulders with a sorrowful look. "I have evidence, but we're getting ahead of ourselves. Please sit down, highness, and let me finish my story.

"When I returned home late last summer, I went looking for the proof Mel told me should be under the floor at the back of your temple. So I couldn't be accused of tampering with any evidence, I invited a pair of my fellow students to go to the so-called chapel with me. Eddie and Diane were studying archeology, the study of old things. They were also working toward doctoral degrees of their own and were quite excited about the idea that there could be relics from some past time beneath the chapel."

"And they accompanied you when you went to study our temple?" Sophie asked.

"Yes," the dark man grinned. "I let them do all the digging. I just sat on a stool beside their dig to provide an impartial witness. We were camped out there beside the golf club for a fortnight as they dug with teaspoons, sifting dirt through screens to search for any miniscule clue. But when they unearthed what I had hoped they would find, they didn't need any screens to separate small amounts of sand."

"You found something big then," Irv stated as a now satisfied Bird climbed into his lap. Hershel, seated across from the king, was bouncing in his seat, anxious for his dark friend to get to the main point of his story. "Yeah," he ejaculated. "Tell'm about the tablets!"

"Yes, thank you, Hersh. That's what I intend to do... Oh, but first, there's that little surprise that I brought for you all." He signaled for Wendy, the downstairs maid, and she supervised as two retainers entered carrying the clinking box Hershel had removed from the time machine. "I think you should have your surprise before I finish my story, Rutherford grinned as Wendy tore open the box lid.

# 🐉 THIRTY-SIX 🐉

From the cardboard carton at his side, Rutherford withdrew a stout green bottle. He snapped his fingers and Wendy placed a corkscrew in the man's hand. The dark scholar made a big show of inspecting the bottle's label. He brought a strange folding knife from his pocket, pulled forth the blade and ran it around the top of the bottle's neck, withdrawing a small circle of metal foil and placing the point of the screw against the flask's cork.

But then, he set the corkscrew down again and held the bottle aloft. "Oh yes, I should tell you a little about this…"

"Is it wine?" Queen Sophie uttered, "Roman wine?"

Rutherford gave a hearty laugh. "It's wine, red wine, but it isn't Roman. It's much better than Roman. This wine has won gold medal awards all over the world! It's California Cabernet wine, from a place on the far side of the land called America. I think you're going to like this. And we will drink this Cabernet in a toast to my success with my studies!"

Bird perked his head up to watch the show. These humans acted so strange sometime that a feline could feel their tension in the air. Now the black man pierced the cork with the hand held screw and drew the stopper out with a flourish. Just as he'd directed them, the castle wait staff entered carrying fancy glass goblets also brought from the future. Wine was poured and Princess Judith started to bring her goblet to her lips. Rutherford stopped her with a look. "First, we must have that toast," he told her. Bird put his front paws on the table and stretched his neck to sniff at the strange glass. Deciding that it wasn't anything interesting for him to eat, he snuggled back into King Irv's lap.

Then, hoisting his own goblet into the air Rutherford said loudly, "To the world's rediscovery of the Jewish history of England!" He lowered the glass to his lips and the others at the feasting board brought their own wine glasses to their mouths for a taste.

Queen Sophie was the first to react. "Oy, God, that is delicious! Irv darling, I love this wine! Thank you Mr., er Doctor Rutherford!" I'm in heaven! Irv, you *must* get me more of this."

Other voices were heard around the table oh-ing, ah-ing and making other yummy noises. But when Hershel set his glass down, he was still bobbing about like a small child in need of a bathroom. "The tablets, Doc, now tell'm about the tablets!"

But King Irv spoke over Hershel's voice as he raised his own goblet. "A toast to our good Doctor Rutherford." Once again, glasses met lips all around the table and the king's men hurried down the line to top up depleting drinks.

"The tablets, the tablets!" Hershel chanted. Bird offered a deep yawn.

"Oh yes," the dark scholar mused tilting his head and rolling his eyes as if trying to remember something. "I did mention my colleagues, Eddie and Diane, did I not? Well, what they lifted from the floorboards of your old temple were a set of well-preserved clay tablets. The first was a tablet that listed the lineage of the Rabbis of your tribe all the way back to before the group lived outside Rome. The other significant clay board listed the line of monarchs that had ruled since they founded your kingdom on British soil." Rutherford's eyes circled the room, meeting the faces of each of the family members seated at the feasting board and ended by making contact with those of King Irv. "The last monarch at the end of the chain," he concluded with a somber face, "is HRH King Irving Benjamin Abrahamson, who was sworn into office and crowned in the year 4066. I must assume that this is you, your majesty and that the date is from the Hebrew calendar. And as there are no further rulers listed, I am left to surmise that your kingdom was either wiped out or united with neighboring peoples to form a larger alliance."

A silence fell over the feast. Irv was wearing a somber look. His queen cast pitying eyes his way. The princess simply appeared confused. Bird leaped from Irv's lap and left the room.

"There's no way you can tell what happened next?" Princess Judith asked the dark skinned man, "Maybe if you dig a little deeper?"

"Diane and Eddie are still working the dig," Rutherford stated in a hopeful tone. "They've dug all around the temple come chapel and unearthed plenty of bones from your graveyard…"

"Unearthed our dead?" Queen Sophie gave an involuntary shudder. "Did they have to do that?"

"They were careful and reverent," Rutherford told her. "They were even able to put names to some of your ancestors by the remains of headstones preserved by a foot or more of sediment and screed." Then, his face growing somber once more, he added. "They found no graves for any of you. Not you, Irv, or you and your good daughter, Queen Sophie. Not even your good prince. I would have thought that your graves, which should have been among the last, would have been the easiest to recognize. An unsolvable mystery,

I guess," he mused.

The ensuing silence was broken after a time by the tacit popping of another cork. The assembly raised their eyes from the half-finished food to see Prince Sol who had entered silently. He was holding a freshly opened bottle of the California wine the staff had hipped him to. "Why so down-hearted here? I thought this was to be a happy gathering? By the way, I apologize for my tardiness, lots to do around the attraction business."

Wendy the maid pulled out a chair for Prince Sol and brought him a platter of food. "Wow," the prince marveled. "Where did we get this wine? I want some of this for Deborah to sell with our pizza!"

With this, some of the pall lifted from the party. No one felt like sharing Rutherford's history lesson, instead turning the conversation to the wine.

"You couldn't afford this wine," Judith laughed at her brother, "Unless you have someone who imports from America."

"America, where's America?"

"It's across a large body of water and over a thousand years into the future," the Merlin smirked. "Doctor Rutherford brought it for us as a surprise."

"Wine from the future?" Prince Sol queried. "How did we get wine from the future?"

"Oh Solly," his sister scolded. "You've been so busy working you probably don't know anything of this. Do you even remember that Hershel built a time machine? No, you probably don't." She leaned over to put an arm around the black scholar's shoulder as he was seated next to her. "Doctor Rutherford brought us award winning wine that's too good to waste on pizza! Besides, he only brought six bottles and we, as a family, are going to keep it to ourselves to enjoy."

"Well," mused the king. "Perhaps I'll share a bottle with Friar Agnello, who thinks he knows all about wine."

"Irving," his queen giggled. "It isn't nice to provoke these Christians! And I'm sure your thoughts of one-upmanship are some kind of sin, maybe a form of envy?"

After the others had gone up to bed, Princess Judith found Rutherford kicking back in the main hall finishing his last glass of the California wine. When she entered the large room, the dark skinned scholar stood, smiled and nodded. "Good evening, Princess."

Judith smiled back. "Please, call me Judith." Then she took a dozen small steps until she was standing close enough to smell the man's cologne. She coyly put her arms around his neck, looked into his deep brown eyes and asked, "Rutherford. Is that your given name or your family name? Should you be formally addressed as doctor…?"

"Johnston," came the man's startled reply, "Doctor Rutherford Percival Johnston." He tried to back up, but the young girl tightened her grip on him with a giggle. "Don't you like girls, Roofie?"

"Roofie?" he choked. "Where did you get 'Roofie?"

The princess relaxed her grip a little and took a step back. "I just decided that's what I want to call you. Do you mind terribly?" She gave the man a conspiratorial wink.

Rutherford had no good answer. He was torn by mixed emotions. Some sly devil inside of him wanted to kiss this bold and beautiful girl, but reason overruled. After all, this was his host, the king's, only daughter. And this young woman was from a whole 'nother place in time and space. He loosed a huge sigh. "Princess Judith," he began.

The girl took another step back and giggled, "Just testing you, *Doctor* Johnston, and teasing too. But you should know that I *do* like you. I like you a lot. And I hope one of these evenings you'll take a walk with me out on daddy's golf course. I think I'd enjoy a bit of conversation with a learned man from the future. And I'd like to find out more about you, Doctor Rutherford P. Johnston!" She then turned on her heel and mounted the stairway up to the sleeping chambers.

# THIRTY-SEVEN

At breakfast the next morning, the princess hardly glanced toward Rutherford, and said no more than a handful of words, mostly to the wait staff. King Irv's fat ginger tom jumped up onto the wide table, attempting to steal bits of food off everyone's plates, but was quickly shooed away. Rutherford didn't know what to think. The king and his Merlin, on the other hand were full of chatter anticipating their morning. The dark scholar had promised to join them in a round of golf, never mind that nine holes on the unfinished course meant playing the three completed fairways thrice. Bird placed his fore paws on Rutherford's thigh with a pitiful hungry look.

As the princess excused herself to go open the pizza stand at the roadside attraction, however, the girl turned to the black scholar with a broad smile and a vicious, telling wink. She looked straight at him and silently mouthed, "Hi Roofie." Whoa! And the scholar's turbulent thoughts went all a-tumble again. His mind was suddenly filled with visions of Judith smiling up at him from beneath the duvet on his narrow bed back home and then peering up from the foaming suds of a hot bath. He shook his nappy head to try and clear it. He mechanically handed one of his unfinished sausages to Bird.

Queen Sophie gave him a questioning look, but Irv and Hershel were so wrapped up discussing how their putting was coming along that they failed to notice Rutherford's distress. Bird the cat had settled all a-purr in the king's lap with his sausage prize. Maybe he should cut his stay here short and head home early, Ruther-ford thought. But what was there waiting back in the future? Lots of hours sitting in the corner of the Castle Golf Club bar drinking too much ale while he waited for this coming interview with the Oxford dons? No, he told himself, I think I'd rather tough it out here!

Thoughts of the princess proved a distraction for the rest of the day, and Rutherford's game suffered accordingly. He hooked his drives into the rough more often than not. His putting was atro-cious, in one instance knocking his ball past the hole, over the edge of the green and into a deep sand trap.

To make matters worse, their game was interrupted halfway through when a small herd of cows meandered onto the second fairway to graze. Irv had to run into the knot of slow animals shout-ing and waving his number two wood to drive them out into the rough so the boys could finish their nine holes.

"You're a regular cowboy," Rutherford told him. "But why do you need so many of these animals? Do you throw a lot of big par-ties and barbeques?"

"Barbeques?"

"Well, outdoor parties where you sear the beef over an open fire."

"Never tried that beyond when the knights and I are out on maneuvers," the king pondered. "Do you think party guests would like eating in the manner of soldiers on a campaign?"

"It's very popular in America, I hear" Rutherford replied, "but you were telling me about this herd of cows."

"It's that dragon my daughter keeps as a pet. Ach, that beast eats what, two, maybe three whole cows a day!"

"Wait a minute, Irv, Princess Judith keeps a pet *dragon*?" The dark skinned scholar tilted his head and gave the king a questioning look. "I've never seen one around the castle. Heck, I've never seen a dragon, period. I didn't even know there was such an animal except in fairy stories."

"So how do you think she cooks her pizza?" the monarch asked.

"Cooks her pizza," came the confused reply. "What has pizza got to do with dragons? You lost me somewhere in this conversation."

"My ovens at the castle weren't hot enough." King Irv told him with a nod that said 'everyone should know this,' so the dragon has to breathe fire on the pizza to melt the cheese properly. And I have had to triple my number of cattle to feed the schtarker!"

Rutherford had to laugh in spite of his dower mood. A pet dragon, and kept by this crazy girl that he thought he was falling in love with? He ended his nine holes with over forty-five strokes. Hershel finished in par and the king scored just one over.

If I'd played this bad back at the Castle course, Rutherford though, I'd be buying drinks for everyone in the county. But here at Warehouse Castle, thankfully, the ale flows freely and no one pays. What would be the cost, he wondered if he was caught fooling around with King Irv's only princess? Would Hershel help him to escape the place, or would the Merlin bar him from the time machine and keep him here to face the music?

The dark skinned man moped around the castle for much of the afternoon, having excused himself from King Irv's company after just two flagons of ale. He wasn't really in the mood for company as he brooded about his emotional dilemma.

Rutherford left the castle for a stroll around the grounds. He walked along the river, where some of the king's men were clearing out the late Mel of the brook's windmill. He moved on past Hershel's cave and out onto the King's Highway where he found himself outside Prince Sol's roadside attraction.

Upon entering, he was greeted by the prince, who began treating *him* as if he were visiting royalty! "Have a glass of wine, doctor, on the house! It's a great honor to have your presence here in my humble business."

"I have been curious," Rutherford replied more to make conversation than anything else.

"You've met our dragon?" Sol asked. "My brave father," he continued with a smirk, "fought, subdued and tamed this ginormous fellow that we call Burny; tamed him enough that we can trust the beast with our tourists and customers, and to bake my sister's pizza dish as well." A couple of pilgrims at the wine bar smiled over at them.

Sure enough there it was, a mountain of gray-green scales with huge wings and a head like an alligator lying down behind a white picket fence. And the monster seemed to be wrestling with a small plush cow, licking the toy and rubbing his head on it. Boy, would this make a story! But then thinking about it, if he ever mentioned a real, live dragon in any scholarly paper, he'd be tossed out of Oxford on his ear before he could teach class one!

Princess Judith, who had been cutting up a pie to serve a small group of traveling monks, recognized Rutherford's voice and looked up with a broad grin. "Welcome, Doctor Johnston," she voiced loudly, then silently mouthed "Roofie."

The dark scholar took the wine and the stool offered by Prince Sol. Judith brought him a large slice of pizza with olives and salted river fish. Rutherford felt his heart catch as a warm feeling came over him. Judith turned from him to serve more customers. He ate his pizza slowly, but quickly finished the less-than-palatable sweet wine and ask Sol if he might have another.

When Rutherford was down to a small bite of crust, there was a lull in the tourist traffic. Prince Sol had gone back into his small office to count the day's take up 'til the minute and record the amount on his parchment. Judith came over to the table where Rutherford sat. She leaned over the man and planted a kiss on his cheek. "So what do you think of *my* pizza, Roofie?"

"It's good, very good," he answered, "but who has been washing his socks in this wine!"

They both burst into laughter, and the princess boldly parked her pretty bottom on the black man's knee. Deborah looked over from the wine bar with a surprised expression that slowly turned into a grin.

"So, how about that walk tonight, eh big fellah? Just meet me down by the stables after dinner. I really want to talk with you. I'd like to, uh, what's that expression of yours that Hershel's been using, 'pick your brains,' is it?"

The princess's use of his turn of phrase started Rutherford laughing again until the girl leaned into him and pressed her forehead against his own. "You're not afraid of me, are you Roofie?" she whispered.

Without thinking, the man blurted out, "No, it's your father I'm afraid of. What he might do if he thought I was fooling around with his only daughter scares the hell out of me."

Deborah turned back to sorting her wine bottles, having heard more than she felt was safe to know.

"Daddy's a pussycat," Judith purred. "I've got daddy wrapped around my little finger. It's mummy that would probably try to slice off your manhood." And then she laughed as a chill ran through Rutherford's body. "So, the stables tonight?" she continued. Without waiting for an answer, the Princess kissed his brow, got to her feet and returned to cleaning her pizza stone.

# 🐉 THIRTY-EIGHT 🐉

Against his better judgment, Rutherford tip-toed stealthily out the back door of the castle after diner and headed toward the stables. He had dressed all in dark colors, black Levis and a navy blue turtleneck shirt, so as to be less visible if someone happened to be watching. Princess Judith was waiting in a fancy gown of pale blue that seemed to push up her ample bosom and was slit up the front to show off her long, slim legs as she walked. She wore a wicked grin, but stepped forward shyly, took the man's elbow and guided him toward the pasture turned first fairway.

"Thanks for indulging me," she told the black man, hugging his arm and rubbing her face against his shoulder. "I'm afraid I've been a bad girl lately and I've embarrassed you, not to mention causing you some inner stress."

"You don't know the half!" Rutherford loudly replied.

"Good!" she stated emphatically. "That would indicate that you *do* like girls. I don't know anything about girls in the future," she pondered, "but I suspect they aren't much different from us girls right here in this time. We all want to find a good fellah that will love us and give us strong, healthy children."

At the mention of children, Rutherford shuddered and pulled away from her embrace. "Oh, don't worry, Roofie," she cooed. "I'm just stating a fact. I'm right, aren't I? And I'm not suggesting that we start making babies right here and now."

The black man blushed so hard his dark skin seemed to be as orange as Bird the ginger cat in the starlight. He let out a large sigh of relief, turned and held the girl out at arm's length, staring at her. Princess Judith spun him back around, took his hand and pulled him along as she began walking again.

"So tell me about this England place in the future," she asked, deftly changing the subject. "You say there's much to learn and people go to school for a long time. Do you think that if I lived in the future, I'd still be going to school? Or are girls just supposed to stay home, cook and mind children?"

"As a princess," he told her, "you would undoubtedly be well educated with many years of university.

"But if I were a commoner?" she queried.

Rutherford gave a deep laugh. "As smart as you are, I'm sure you'd be in line for many years of study." Princess Judith smiled at this.

Her questions went on, about how people in Rutherford's time lived, what villages were like in the future, what people ate and more. This new line of conversation put Rutherford somewhat at ease and he found he enjoyed sharing words with this beautiful young lass. He told her about fancy five-star restaurants where folks went to eat high priced meals. They had strolled twice around the existing length of the golf course making small talk and ended back by the stables where they had begun, just as a thin sliver of moon cleared the treetops.

Suddenly, the young princess spun around to face him, locked his head between her two hands, stretched up on tip toes and kissed him hard on the mouth, then just as suddenly, she twirled from his grasp and bolted for the castle shouting, "Sleep tight, Roofie!"

In spite of his worries about being found out, Rutherford continued meeting Princess Judith each night after the evening meal had been finished. For several nights, the girl was a prim and proper lady. They spoke of the future and no mention was made of the girl's promising kiss that had ended their first date.

Then, on the last night before the scholar was scheduled to return to the future, their relationship heated up. At the far end of the third fairway, Princess Judith grabbed Rutherford's shoulders, caught him off balance and they both tumbled into a sand trap beyond the green. The princess wrestled his body over until she was on top and had him pinned in the sandy depression. She began to offer a tame kiss, but quickly had parted the man's lips to seek out his tongue. Biology took control and Rutherford was returning her soulful kiss. All fears were instantly forgotten as their breathing quickened and hands traveled over both their prone bodies.

Just as quickly as it had begun, Judith released him and stood up, looking down over him, her breath still coming in short rapid bursts. "That," she panted, "is a promise of what you will find when you return again." She turned her most powerful smile on him in the pale moonlight. "And Roofie, you *will* be coming back. I know you will, because that kiss is going to haunt you until you return to me!"

Rutherford sat halfway up in the sand, leaning back on his elbows to stare at her. "Girl," he breathed, "you are even smarter than I had given you credit for! I'll be back. And while I'm gone maybe you should see about getting your mother wrapped around your little finger as well!"

Judith didn't turn up for breakfast the following morning. King Irv announced to all that his daughter had told him she had things to catch up on at the roadside attraction and would simply nibble on the previous day's cold, leftover pizza for her morning meal.

Hershel was waiting right after the meal was finished to take his dark skinned friend back to future times, so there was no chance of seeing the princess once more before his departure. Rutherford was disappointed, but there was nothing he could do. He marched to the Merlin's time machine like a condemned man to the gallows.

## THIRTY-NINE

After Rutherford's departure, King Irv fell into the doldrums. He missed his conversations with the learned man from the future and was exceedingly curious about what the man had said of him being the last monarch of Warehouse Castle. Was something terrible going to befall his now serious and dedicated son after the young man had made such strides? And why couldn't these future people find the graves of himself, his wife and his family? It was almost too much to reflect on, but just the same, King Irv found himself obsessed by it. He stroked the large orange tomcat in his lap. "Do you know anything about this mystery, Bird? Ach, if only you could talk to me. I understand that cats are very wise creatures. Those Egyptians in the Torah believed you to be Gods even."

His servants completed the fourth hole in his golf course a week later and he threw himself into rigid golf practice to divert his thoughts. Once he felt he'd mastered the new fairway and green, he invited Hershel, the Rabbi and Friar Agnello to make up a foursome and try it out as well.

Bird stalked them for the first couple holes. On the second green, the large ginger tom raced across the short fescue batting Irv's ball off into a sand trap. His partners joked about King Irv having to play his ball where it lies, but in the end they allowed him to replace it on the green where Bird had attacked it without taking a penalty stroke on the score card.

One of his gardeners approached them as they came off the

third green the morning of their game to announce that the fifth hole, a shorter distance and lower par than the others, would be ready to play within a fortnight. Irv tipped the man a brass coin at which the gardener bowed low and thanked him profusely.

The king came in with a score of three under par to beat his friends. He silently thanked God that he had put in so much practice time before challenging his buddies. It had been a perfect day for golf and the gentle breeze felt so nice that Irv invited all to hang around for awhile. He summoned someone from the kitchen staff to bring them all drinks, ale for himself and Hershel, a bottle of good wine for the two men of God. He slipped one of his retainers a hand-full of brass coins to go out to the roadside attraction and fetch a pizza with everything to go and bring it back for his guests.

"It's a funny thing-a," Friar Agnello said when the pizza arrived. "Everyone-a says this pizza, it comes from Roma... But I don't-a remember anything like-a this when I lived there."

Hershel shot the king a wink and they both smiled. "Maybe it's from that island place south of Roma," Rabbi Weiss put in suppressing a laugh, "Sicilia is it called?"

"That would make-a sense," the perplexed padre said. Bird put two paws up on the man of Christ's knee with a loud purr but then turned and settled in Irv's lap, purring loudly.

"So when can we expect another visit from our doctor friend, Rutherford?" the Rabbi asked King Irv.

"Rutherford? The man's a doctor?" Friar Agnello asked. "You mean the black-a fellow? The man who knows about golf?"

The king shot them all a clouded look with a shake of the head.

"Doctor Rutherford is supposed to be a secret, at least from the surrounding kingdoms, Let's just say he's a pilgrim from some far away land called England," King Irv told his friend Giovanni Agnello with a dismissive wave.

"He brought us a gift of this fine wine." The grinning Rabbi Weiss added.

"It is an exceptional-a vintage." The friar remarked. "I was-a gonna inquire about it. Is this-a something that your-a prince is gonna start serving in his-a little café? It would-a certainly be an improvement over that-a Dragon Blood plonk!"

"Ah, it's really rare stuff," Hershel told the friar. "Quite pricey, it comes from very far away, much farther away than Roma." Under his breath he whispered, "About a thousand years away," rolling his eyes heavenward.

"The church would-a contribute a gold-a bar or two for a cask of this-a here stuff," said the priest, smacking his lips, "just-a saying…"

"From what I understand this wine only comes in bottles," King Irv related with a serious mask. "But if I get any more, I'll surely donate a bottle to your church, Giovanni."

"Ah," the friar hesitated. "Could-a you maybe make it a personal gift-a just-a to me? If-a it is as rare as you say, I don't-a wish to share it with-a my brothers at-a the church."

When his guests had left Irv remained in his comfortable patio chair, his cat stretched out along his thigh, enjoying the little buzz he had from the ale and his victorious golf game. He must have dozed off for a moment. He woke with a start to find his daughter,

Princess Judith, grinning down at him. Bird also noticed the princess. He lifted his orange head for her to pet, brought up his white chin for a chuck, then bolted for the stable area.

"Oh good, daddy, you're awake. I've got a small favor to ask. Some little thing you can do for Solly and me."

"Anything for my wonderful children," Irv smiled. "You know you are both the light of my life and life's greatest blessing. Anything you ever desire, just ask!"

"I'll have to think about that, pop," she replied with a calculating gaze. "But for right now, could you stop by the roadside attraction tomorrow for a few minutes? Oh, and wear one of your special regal robes and that handsome gold crown of yours."

A perplexed look spread across King Irv's countenance. "Am I to meet some visiting earl or monarch?" he inquired. "Is there a reason I should be so dressed up?"

"Just as a favor to me, pop," she grinned, taking a seat on her father's knee and hugging him tightly.

"Tomorrow, that would be Tuesday," King Irv said thoughtfully. "I don't believe I have anything important on the royal calendar. Any particular time?"

"Oh, let's say just before lunch time. I'll have some pizza for you and some ale as well so you don't have to endure Deborah's dreadful wine!" The girl thought for a moment and continued. "Did you know that Doctor Rutherford tried some of our Dragon's Piss?" She gave a hearty laugh and told her father, "After tasting it Rutherford asked me if someone had been washing their socks in it! Isn't that a hoot?"

## FORTY

O n route to his children's business the next day, Irv noticed a scroll nailed up on a thick oak tree beside the King's Highway proclaiming "Tewsday at high noon, come to the roadside attraction to meet and greet HRH King Irving and bear witness as he performs the Blessing of the Pizzas!" What was this? He chuckled to himself. It must be another of Prince Sol's brilliant marketing ideas. He reflected again on just how intelligent his children were. But why had they not simply told him what they were planning? Did they think that he might consider blessing pizzas somewhere beneath his station? Oh his brilliant, yet at the same time, foolish children!

Just over the rise, Irv could see a crowd gathered before the attraction's stout facade. Prince Sol appeared from out of the trees across the highway. "This way, father," he whispered loudly. "We have so many good people gathered out front that I think I had better sneak you in the back way, eh, for your safety." The prince crossed the road, took his father by the elbow and led him on a circuitous route around boulders to Burny's pen, where he guided his father behind the wine bar and through the heavy drapes into his private office.

"I'm going to say a few words to your gathered subjects," he told his father, "Then, I'll announce you, and Judith will lead you out from behind curtains."

Ducking through the hanging beads of the prince's office, King Irv recognized many of the village merchants in the first few rows at the roadside attraction along with other local farmers and some prominent families. They all appeared jubilant and happy to be here to see their king blessing pizza. Was pizza really that special? Well, he thought, it *had* brought some prosperity to the people of his realm. Folks from far and wide that had stopped to try this exotic dish *did* tend to linger and shop in the village just beyond his castle walls. The Wholesale Kingdom was, after all, the only place in the local world where pizza could be sampled. He suddenly felt very special as he called forth Rabbi Weiss from the assembly to aid in this so-called blessing.

Looking back through Burny's enclosure, he saw that Princess Judith had a number of extra baking stones lined up along Burny's pit and a stack of pre-baked pizzas waiting as well. Irv turned back to his audience, nodding to the good Rabbi that it was time to start the ceremony.

"As your King and humble royal servant," he began, "it gives me great pleasure to appear before you today along with our good teacher, Rabbi Weiss, to bless this new culinary delight re-created right here in our own kingdom and available only here at the Warehouse Castle's roadside attraction. I'm speaking of the delight that has come to us from far away Rome, a unique dish that combines so many exotic flavors all rolled into one dish and is known to us as... pizza!"

A loud cheer rose from the assembly. People were shouting "we love pizza" and "long live King Irv!"

When the applause had died down, Princess Judith was standing by King Irv's side. "As a thank you to all his loyal subjects that have supported our wise and brave monarch for all these years," she shouted, "Our good King Irv has asked that I give a free slice of our best pizza and a glass of Dragon Wine to each and every one of you right after his majesty and our good Rabbi have given their blessings to this food which awaits behind me! Please, everyone form a queue and each of you will be served in turn. Our dragon, Burny, will continue to bake pies while you are served to insure that we shan't run short and everyone will get a taste!"

Another cheer rose from the crowd and a complement of Irv's finest knights entered to organize the formation of a line from the front viewing row right out the entrance and into the street.

King Irv remained for over an hour, kissing the hands of the women and bowing to the men. A small number of his subjects mentioned favors they would appreciate. About a dozen mentioned that leaves falling in the autumn past had blocked drains to the river or that some tree roots had poked up along the village high street posing a trip hazard to their horses. King Irv made a note of their concerns and promised that he would personally see to the remedy of these circumstances.

The king returned home that evening feeling happy and satisfied. He sat back on his favorite couch in the main hall, having pulled the opposing divan close so he could put his feet up on it. Bird leaped into his lap, curled into his crotch and purred loudly. His servants brought ale and Morrie entered with his lute to entertain with a catchy tune or two.

When Morrie bowed out, Princess Judith came in and sat herself down at her father's side. Bird immediately jumped into Judith's lap, stretched out up her sweater and gave her face a lick before returning to balance on King Irv's knee.

"Thank you, daddy! It has just been a magic day! I'm so happy. Do you know how many pizza slices we gave away? And I'm sure some of the villagers who have never been to our roadside attraction before will start coming back regularly!"

The princess snuggled into her father's side. "Pop? Yesterday you said, "Anything I ever desire, just ask. Did you mean that, pop?"

When she called him 'pop' Irv just melted anyway. "Of course I meant it. Didn't I say it? What, am I not a guy to stick by his word?"

"Well…" Judith said, "What if I had a boyfriend…" Bird's slitted eyes popped open and his tail began sailing rhythmically to and fro.

"Are you kidding," Irv sputtered, "you're too young to be thinking about boys, are you kidding me? A boyfriend?"

"Well," the princess breathed again, "let's just say that there was this boy that I was interested in…" Bird rested his head back on the king's knee and closed his eyes. Nobody asked cats for their opinion.

"I don't think I like where this conversation is going," Irv replied testily.

"Oh, pop!" his daughter said, "I'm a big girl! Don't you remember I had my bat mitzvah almost two years ago?"

"If some boy in the village has been putting his hands on you I'll…"

"You'll do what, daddy? If you're going to be like that maybe I can't confide in you… You're my closest, dearest friend whom I've always thought I could come to with any problem." Bird perked up again, turning his head to stare at the princess.

"Ach, what am I saying! Yes, please talk to me. It's just that you're my little girl…You'll always be my little girl. I just don't think you're ready yet to learn so much about life. Is there something you need to be telling me? I'm ready to listen."

"Nothing like that now," the princess giggled. "I just wanted to be sure that, when the time comes, I can confide in you. And maybe you'll be able to talk with mummy to. She's never been as understanding as you are, pops."

# 🐉 FORTY-ONE 🐉

O n a drizzly morning with winter approaching, Hershel sent Ezekiel, one of the golf course gardeners, to ask King Irv if he might find a minute to stop by his cave for a little talk. "Is the Merlin ill?" the monarch asked Ezekiel as the man doffed his hat. "This seems a most unusual request. Kings are supposed to summon their people to *them*, not the other way around."

"Sir, Hershel said nothing more to me," the gardener answered, fidgeting nervously with his hat. "He looked to be in good health."

"Well thank you, Ezekiel," Irv said with a benevolent smile. "And, my good man, it is not *Sir* Hershel. Hershel is my *Merlin*, not a knight. A different office all together."

"I stand corrected, my liege!" Ezekiel bowed low before his king, covered his head and scampered for the door. Irv eased the purring Bird off his lap and stood to look for his winter coat.

King Irv found Hershel in the depths of his deep cavern standing under the light of three bright torches and staring at the open suitcase containing that silver paper stuff Rutherford referred to as 'pound notes.' "I don't use much of this stuff," the Merlin said without looking up when he heard Irv's approach. "I mean I might arm myself with a couple twenty pound things when I go to play golf or something. Rutherford usually pays for my drinks and when I stay for a few days, he lets me sleep on the couch in his flat." Hershel turned his head to look at Irv. "This is probably very valuable stuff. I'd like to pledge it to the kingdom, but I don't know if you'd be able to do any more with it than I can."

"This is true." His king told him with a sigh and an extremely serious face. "It is probably worth a small kingdom or two in the future, but what can we do with it here?

"Well, I was thinkin'" Hershel began. "Maybe if we talk to Rutherford next time we see him. He might know of a way we can send this stuff to the future and get some of the value of it back for us here."

"I don't know how that might work." King Irv stated.

"Well," drawled Hershel, "maybe he could keep us supplied with that California wine and tinned ale."

"The worth of a kingdom in fancy wine and drink?" Irv shook his head. "That doesn't sound like any kind of a deal. We don't even have a use for the empty ale tins anymore."

"Well, don't you think we should talk to the man? He's a really smart guy. We can show him what we got and he might be able to help."

"Well, yes," Irv thought out loud. "It would do no harm to show him this paper stuff and ask his opinion."

Hershel was gone for a few days. When he returned he made a bee line for the castle and the company of his king.

"Rutherford says he's got a fortnight off from school for those up-coming Christian holidays. He's asked me to bring him back here as he doesn't have any plans for Christ Mass or the New Year. So maybe we can have a little confab with him about that money stuff."

"That sounds fine," Irv told him stroking the purring Bird that occupied his lap, "but how about we have one of my servants drag that paper stuff up here to the castle. It looks like it might snow sometime soon and you know how cold it gets in that cave of yours!"

"Yeah, okay," Hershel answered. "You know most of the time I'm so busy inventing things and trying out new formulas for turning old ale cans into gold, I don't even notice."

"And now that I'm forewarned, Sophie and Judith will have plenty of time to plan a very special banquet for us. Do we know if the good doctor is a Christian? Well, just in case we'll have a sort of combination Hanukkah and Christ Mass party. It should be fun!"

"I'll be lookin' forward to that," the Merlin intoned. "Maybe we could invite Rabbi Weiss and Giovanni Agnello too, that is if the friar ain't too busy around the village church over in Berten-on-Cherwell."

Irv was surprised at how excited Princess Judith became at the mention of a holiday party for the good Doctor Rutherford. The girl was off like a shot, assembling staff to see to the procurement of some large pheasants and winter vegetables. Judith spent an hour in the cellar inspecting jars of jams and preserves the staff had canned last spring, selecting the finest of those for the kitchen staff to bring up to the pantry for the big dinner. By the next day, she had Wendy polishing up their special silver menorah and Jeevestein sent off to the village to buy vanilla scented candles to put in it. During the day, at her pizza kitchen, she distractedly mulled over recipes for special cakes and pies. Fortunately, the inclement weather curtailed much of their business by keeping all but the most hearty pilgrims off the highway.

Over a glass of the remaining California wine that evening, Queen Sophie asked Irv, "Oy, what has lit such a fire under that daughter of ours? All she talks about is this coming holiday feast. She's sent her best gowns to be cleaned and pressed. If I didn't know better, I'd say she was acting like a girl in love!"

# 🐉 FORTY-TWO 🐉

When Hershel the Merlin's time machine materialized through the fog on a cold December morning, Princess Judith ran forth from the castle after her father to meet the contraption's arrival. Rutherford bounded out of the vehicle with his customary big grin, maybe even a few lumens brighter than King Irv remembered it being. He reached back into the cab and pulled out a large and funny black hat which he placed on King Irv's head. He pulled it down and squared it over the monarch's brow.

"And what would this be?" Irv laughed "I don't mind a few flakes of snow on my bald pate."

"Remember when you were rounding up those cows on the golf course and I called you a cowboy?" the good doctor chuckled. "Well, *that* is a ten-gallon cowboy hat, all the way from the wild west of America. The same California place where they make the Cabernet wine! And I brought you some western spurs as well, so next time you can put them on your boots and chase the cows on your horse." The king and the scholar hugged. They both laughed at these silly presents.

From behind King Irv's shoulder, Princess Judith caught Rutherford's attention. She made a clouded face and mouthed "Roofie" silently, then softly spoke, "What about me, anything for me?"

The black man's laugh grew in intensity as he reached back into the time machine. When he turned back toward Princess Judith, he had a small box in his hand that was wrapped in modern holiday paper of red and green. The princess took the offered package and broke into a very wide grin. She shook the box next to her ear to attempt a guess at what it might contain. "Thank you, doctor," she blushed turning her gaze toward the grass at her feet.

"Uh, it's Professor now," the man beamed. "I've been offered a job teaching at Oxford, so I'm still a doctor, but now I'm also going to be a professor, which I think is a much more important title."

"Well congratulations, professor!" King Irv shouted stepping between his daughter and the dark man to shake his hand. Hershel drove his way between them as well to congratulate Rutherford. Then a porter showed up to carry the newly anointed professor's luggage to his chambers back at the castle.

As the king and his Merlin were sneaking a peak into the time machine to see if there was more wine, ale or possibly new golf balls, Rutherford leaned close to the princess. "I have another small present for you as well," he whispered. "But it's a surprise and I'll give it to you later, when we're alone." The princess gave him a resolute nod.

Princess Judith was a bundle of nerves as she oversaw the setting of the large banquet table and the preparation of the many dishes in the kitchen. She couldn't recall ever feeling this excited and took a deep breath to calm the host of butterflies that seemed to fill her small, flat tummy.

She could hear Rutherford's happy laughter mixed with the other male guests and her father sharing a pre-dinner drink out in the main hall. "Please God," she prayed, "make this the most fantastic feast that there has ever been, ever!" Bird was curled up on the hearth of the dining hall fireplace. He didn't like sharing his human with as many other people as were gathered in the big hall.

Judith was wearing the fragrant perfume that Rutherford had brought her as a gift. He had told her that in the future this tiny flask of scent was more valuable than a case of the special California wine which, by the way, he had brought as a special gift for her mother, the queen. And what could be this other pressie he mentioned? He didn't have any more large boxes with him that she could see.

The meal was perfect. Rabbi Weiss was in attendance, but Friar Agnello had sent his regrets. As they were being seated, Wendy carried in the case of California wine, wrapped in the same bright colorful paper as Judith's perfume had worn. Kitchen help were immediately there with the fancy future goblets to set before each guest and a corkscrew which was presented to the new professor. Queen Sophie was very pleased when she'd torn away the bright paper, opened the box and handed a bottle to Rutherford for opening. Bird had been banned from the banquet and sat out in the stables plotting his revenge.

The pheasant had been cooked just right, tender but still full of flavor. Rutherford had asked for a second helping of Judith's rhubarb pie, remarking that he'd never tasted better. When she'd said she made it herself, he'd sent an especially loving look her way. The princess couldn't wait to share another moonlight walk with him on the golf course, which now had seven finished holes winding east of the brook along the river.

As they were finishing the last of their afters, Morrie the Jester came strolling down the hall from the kitchens with his lute singing, "I got spurs that jingle, jangle, jingle, as I go riding merrily along. Oh Nellie Belle, oh Nellie Belle...."

"And what would be the meaning of this song?" the king inquired.

"It's a western cowboy song, from America, your highness," Rutherford chuckled. "Morrie can saddle up a horse with you when you go chasing cows and he can sing this to you. You do, now, have such jingle-jangle spurs and the cowboy hat as well."

"Oh for peter's sake," scoffed the monarch. "Don't you know it's a crime to mock the regent of this realm?"

"So lock me up in your dungeon, Irv. Just make sure you feed me on this fine pheasant, those tasty brussel sprouts and plenty of your good princess's rhubarb pie!"

"She made the entire meal herself, actually," Queen Sophie interjected as she wiped her lips on one of the fine, sky blue linen serviettes. "Quite a talented girl is our little Princess Judith."

Rutherford started to say, "You're telling me!" but caught himself and turned his words to, "you're te, uh, you must be very proud."

The king and queen didn't seem to catch his almost slip-of-the-tongue as they beamed at their only daughter.

# ❦ FORTY-THREE ❦

Everyone wanted to talk to Rutherford after dinner. They went on endlessly, the Rabbi asking about the man's spiritual beliefs, Hershel with questions about how harsh the winter might be back in England and if the golf course had been buried in snow as the castle's fairways and greens had been here. Would they never grow tired and leave this man to her?

The Rabbi was the first to stifle a yawn and excuse himself. At some point Bird had strolled in and parked his ginger bulk in front of the fire waiting for Irv to pay him some attention. Finally Hershel observed that it was getting late and he needed his beauty rest.

As soon as Irv and Sophie retired Rutherford went through the kitchens and out the back door to the stables. He noticed that it was a new moon overhead and wondered if starlight would be enough to guide them around the course without tripping and falling on some exposed root or stone.

Approaching the horse barn, he saw that the princess was wearing a heavy coat. He felt a little shiver himself. Maybe it was simply too cold for a walk on this night. When he got close to Judith, she reached out, grabbed him and pulled him into the stables, kicking the door closed behind him. In an instant, she threw open her winter coat and was standing before him in her birth suit. Rutherford's knees turned to water and a loud moan escaped from his throat.

"Quiet, silly," Judith laughed softly. "Do you want to wake up the whole castle?" Then she covered his mouth with her open mouth to prevent his uttering another sound. Rutherford's knees continued their buckling and soon the couple was lying on the straw floor of the first stall. Princess Judith, who had landed on top of the large black man, pulled back from their lingering kiss and whispered, "It's cold in here, Roofie. You'd better do something to warm up my little body."

After some time, when their heart rates and breathing had returned to near normal, Judith propped herself up on one elbow, her breasts swaying close to her lover's face. She cast a serious look down into his dark eyes. "Roofie," she purred. "I want to run away to the future with you. I've made up my mind. I want to feel this good forever!"

The black man's look of surprise turned into a happy grin. "You serious about that?" he asked. "What do you think your parents will say?"

"Roofie, I've honestly never felt as happy as I've been these past months since we started walking and talking together. I know we haven't spent that much time in each other's company and I know there's a lot I still have to learn about you. But I know enough... When I'm with you I feel so full of joy, so special? Yes, special!"

Rutherford chuckled softly. Could this really be happening? "And your father? What will he say?"

"So I haven't a clue what your future time might be like," Judith rocketed on as though she hadn't heard him, "but if you're there, I know it will be fabulous. Do you want to share your life with me, Roofie?" A cloud passed over the princess's pretty face. "You don't already have a girlfriend where you're from do you?"

Rutherford gave another contented chuckle. "You know the other surprise I told you I was saving for later?" He reached behind him to where his clothing had fallen in his haste to get naked, found his tweed sports coat and rummaged through the pockets, finally bringing forth a tiny cube wrapped in more of that holiday paper. As he handed it to her, he told her, "I was going to save this for later, like maybe just before I left but right now has just become the most appropriate time I could have wished for."

Princess Judith pulled her other arm and one knee out from under the scholar's body. She sat up cross-legged tearing at the colorful paper, her sizable breasts swaying provocatively with the ripping motion. The torn paper revealed a small, dark velvet box. She stared at the cube for a moment and Rutherford told her, "It opens. Have a look at what's inside."

Judith tilted up the lid and squealed so loud in her joy that she might have been heard as far away as Vaudeville or Berten-on-Cherwell.

"What was that a little while ago about waking up the whole castle?" the dark scholar whispered with a wide grin. They sat listening for a few beats, but heard no one approaching.

"It's It's, ah, It's a ring!" the princess stuttered breathlessly.

"An engagement ring, you do have engagement rings in your time, don't you? It just seems appropriate," Rutherford scolded, "that before I whisk you away into the future I should at least ask you to marry me!"

"Oh Roofie," Judith exclaimed in a softer voice, tears forming at the corner of her lovely eyes, "I don't know what to say! Of course we have engagement rings here, and wedding rings too."

"How about 'yes?' That would be a nice word for the occasion." The man pressed her.

"Yes," the girl breathed softly, then a decibel louder, "Oh, yes, Roofie, yes! I want to be your wife!"

She was crying big time as she fell back across the dark professor and began placing kisses all over his face, neck and shoulders, finally finding his mouth with her own wide open mouth and tongue.

As the happy couple began dressing to sneak back into the castle, Rutherford asked again, "What about your parents? Do you think your father would let me live long enough to attend the wedding if he knew what we've been doing here tonight?

"*I'll* handle daddy," Judith purred confidently. "I've already had one talk with him…"

"My God, you didn't mention me by name did you?" Rutherford blurted out with fear in his eyes.

The princess giggled again. "No, I just kinda asked him some 'what if' questions, like what if I had a boyfriend. At first he started shouting about me being too young, but then we came to a bit of an understanding. I think I'll tell daddy about us, but I'll let him explain to mummy. Like maybe after you go back. By the time you return to get me, it should all be ironed out."

From the hay loft, two bright yellow eyes watched the departing couple. If only we cats had the gift of speech, Bird thought to himself. Oh, the stories I could tell! Then he closed his eyes and went back to sleep.

# 🐉 FORTY-FOUR 🐉

Rutherford was a bundle of nerves the next morning as he kept his appointment with King Irv and Hershel. He wasn't sure why they'd requested a private audience, but he didn't like the way that big ginger tomcat of the king's had been following him and staring his way all morning. He'd never believed in witches or magic, but if there was someplace it could exist, it would be in these ancient times. Was that darn cat somehow psychically connected to his majesty?

He gave a soft knock at the private basement doorway as Hershel had instructed, then hearing the king's musical baritone shout "Come," he marched into the semi-dark claustrophobic space.

"Thanks for joining us," the king said conspiratorially. "This is a secret meeting. No one else knows you're here do they?"

Rutherford felt his manhood shrinking with fear, but replied in a full voice, "No, your highness. I've told no one." Were they ready to kill him and hide the body?

"Nothing to worry about, Professor," the king told him. "You look a bit pale, like maybe you didn't get enough sleep? Hershel, would I hurt this man? He's like a son to me!"

The dark scholar felt a little catch in his throat and his head grew light. How could they know? Had someone been following the princess? Spying on her? Maybe the cat *was* the monarch's extra set of eyes?"

Then Hershel set two torches on the wall alight and the king threw back a heavy blanket that was covering something on the cold stone floor.

Rutherford's jaw dropped as he gazed on an old broken American Tourister flight case folded open and overflowing with fifty and one-hundred pound notes. My God, he thought, had his friend Hershel robbed the local Barclays' Bank on one of his trips?

"Well, at least you've got some color returning to your face," King Irv observed. "So you see before you the problem I have. Hershel tells me that this paper stuff is worth a fortune in the future you come from, but it's only useful for starting fires or stuffing pillows around here."

"We've been thinkin'," the Merlin put in, "maybe you could bring some of this stuff to the future and trade it for gold or wine or something that might be useful to us here. Any ideas you have would be appreciated."

"Trade this for gold? I suppose it could be done, but that would be a hell of a lot of gold, a really heavy load for that machine of yours, Hersh.

"Where did this come from, anyway? It looks like half-a-million pounds or more! Where did you get this?"

"Ah, I'd rather not say," the Merlin began.

"Listen, Hershel. We want this man to help us," the king reasoned, "I think we should be honest with him. You think this guy is going to have you arrested when you go back to play golf with him?"

"Well, I dunno," the Merlin mused.

"How about I tell him what you told me," King Irv reasoned.

"Okay, I'll tell the tale. I was the one there at the scene." Hershel turned to face Rutherford. "It was an accident. I want you should know I meant nobody no harm. My very first trip to your time, like I was still learning about how to fly my machine and didn't know exactly what I was doing…

"Well, I landed on top of some guy and I guess I broke his neck. When I checked him he was seriously dead. Then I notice he's got this bag with him." The Merlin kicked at the suitcase for emphasis. "I was frightened and confused, so like, I load the dead guy and his case into the machine and I came home. I stared at this case thing for days before I got up the nerve to bust it open and see what was inside."

"All that money." Rutherford mused shaking his head.

"Yeah, well each of these papers says it's so many pounds but a handful of it weighs less than a hummingbird. It made me very curious." Hershel smiled at the dark man.

"He was curious enough," King Irv interrupted, "that he put on this dead guys clothes and tried going back to where he landed on this guy."

"Yeah, and you know the rest, Professor. When I went back wearing this guy's outfit, that's when I ran into you in the club bar."

Rutherford rested his chin thoughtfully on the palm of his hand. "That's quite a story! I seem to remember someone going missing around that time. He was some kind of drug dealer. The local cops were glad to see the back of him, happy that he disappeared, I mean. No one was sorry to see him gone. The man must have just collected some kind of score."

"A score?" Hershel questioned, "You mean like a low golf score? At night?"

The dark professor laughed. "No, I mean a large criminal pay-off. In modern times when a thief gets away with a large sum of money, they call it a 'score.' Obviously this man you ran into didn't get to spend any of his score."

"So can you help us? Is there something we can do with this, uh, what did you call it? Money?"

"I will have to give that some thought," Rutherford told them. "If I suddenly show up with a large cache of cash like this, it would look very suspicious. I would have to exchange it a little at a time so they don't think I'm some kind of robber or drug dealer."

"And a drug dealer would be?" asked King Irv.

"Oh, that is another topic completely. In my time, many people aren't happy just to get squiffy with a glass of ale or wine. Some-one invented pills that make you, ah what's that word you use? Mashuga. And plants, there are plants that people smoke to change their thinking."

"Crazy pills? Plants to smoke? Is that legal? The Merlin in-quired.

"No," came the professor's resounding reply. "It is *not* legal. And that is why criminals, like this man you ran over, can make so much money selling pills and weed."

"Well, I guess we shouldn't need this money all at once," Irv said thoughtfully. "Just let us know if you can come up with an answer."

"I guess I'll just leave the stuff here," Hershel announced. "I got some things I'm working on in my laboratory. Can we meet up later for a tankard or two?"

"Certainly, Hershel," came the king's reply. "Say around mid afternoon?"

"See you then," the Merlin replied already halfway out of the small room.

King Irv made to hold the door for Rutherford while sweeping out his hand in a motion that the scholar should precede him.

Rutherford hung back shifting his eyes around anxiously and wringing his hands. "Ah, your majesty, could I talk to you for just a minute?"

"Shouldn't we go upstairs and talk over a pint of ale," asked the king.

"Well," the professor hesitated. "This is kind of secret, well maybe not secret, but personal, if you know what I mean, really personal."

"No, I don't think I know what you mean," the king stated suspiciously. As he said this, Bird strolled into the dark space and sat down atop the pile of pound notes in the suitcase. He shot piercing, accusing eyes at Rutherford and the man began to sweat in spite of the chilly temperature of the basement room.

"Ah, Jesus, I guess I better get this over with," Rutherford sighed. "There won't be any better time."

"Is there something wrong with my hospitality," the king asked. "Have my people said or done something to offend?"

"No, that's just it," the dark scholar wailed. "You've all been too good to me. You've welcomed me as though I was part of your family and now I feel like I may have betrayed you in a sense."

"You have, as far as I know, always been a perfect gentleman, dear professor," the king said with a slight bow of his head.

"I wish that were so," Rutherford lamented shaking his head. "Oh hell, your highness," the man returned the kings bow only much deeper, almost touching the stones before Irv with his forehead. "I hope you won't be angry... ah, I want to marry your daughter!" he finally blurted out. "I'm in love with your delightful Princess Judith!"

The monarch's face clouded and a crimson blush started on his forehead spreading downward. "You what!" he screamed. Then the tall ruler turned and slammed a fist into the heavy oaken door to the cellar.

"Ouch," he proclaimed and began a dance around the room clutching one injured hand with the other. Rutherford wished that he could somehow shrink very small and disappear into the surrounding stones.

Suddenly, the king was laughing. He danced over and threw an arm around the dark scholar's shoulder. "I should have guessed that something was up," he said, giving the dark man a sort of sideways hug, "the way that girl has been acting lately. You know she came to me the other day asking how I'd feel if she had a boyfriend. I suspected that one of the vassals might be trying to have his way with her."

Rutherford gave a tacit "Sir?"

"Understand I'm not thrilled with this," the king stated thoughtfully. "But I should have known it would happen some-day. Children *do* grow up, no matter how we'd like to have them as children forever.

"I don't know what the Queen will say to all this." he contin-ued. "I'll have to have a solemn talk with her. But I don't suppose there's much we can do if you've both have made your minds up."

"Thank you sir," the professor said in a hushed voice.

"But do give this some time." The king added in a loud, sure voice. "I'll do what I can, but I don't want anyone taking a shot on an impulse. I'll give my blessing *only* if you'll promise to give the princess time to be sure of her heart and mind!"

"Agreed, sire," Rutherford told him, turning to go back to what he hoped to be his future father-in-law's hug.

# FORTY-FIVE

The king and the scholar locked the cellar door on the suitcase full of cash and moved their meeting up to the great hall. Bird followed close on their heels and when the two men sat, Bird claimed his rightful place on King Irv's lap. A servant heard their entrance and shimmered in with two large tankards.

"So," King Irv began, "I know Queen Sophie will ask me, do you expect my daughter to give up her faith?"

Rutherford gave the king a broad smile, "Actually, Irv, I've been studying about Judaism back at school. Oxford has a Hebrew Studies program and I've spent my recent Saturdays at Torah study, with a Rabbi from the Oxford Chabad Society. If Judith wants me to I'll gladly convert to Judaism. I've been thinking about becoming Jewish for some time anyway." He gave the king a confident look. "My parents sent me to a hell, fire and damnation Christian church when I was little. Everybody talked about how happy Jesus made them, but nobody ever smiled. They spoke of peace and love, but they were always fighting and condemning the others around them, so I had simply given up on religion."

"I think this will put the queen's mind somewhat at rest." King Irv smiled.

"So you, here at Warehouse castle," Rutherford asked. "Your kingdom seems very informal and relaxed. The history I've read always speaks about kings of old continually battling for their honor or trying to grab more land for themselves, I know you have knights and I see them practicing their skills around the property, but I've seen no battles or even talk of battle. And things are so calm and friendly here."

"Ach," Irv answered. "We are a peaceful people, a peace loving people. We try to get along with everyone. We have our faith, but we don't force it on our neighbors. Live and let live, you know? We keep to ourselves, mostly. God has blessed us in so many ways, why make waves?"

"Wow, I'd like to have put that into my thesis."

"Well, it is good simply that you have assured our kingdom some small part in the world's memory. What more could we ask?" The monarch sipped contentedly from his ale.

"It seems like a perfect life to me," the dark scholar agreed. "Drink ale and play golf. If only my life was that simple… Maybe I should just stay here with Judith!"

"Oy, stay here?" The king was startled. "You would stay here? What? We don't need a teacher here, we've got our Rabbi. And how would I explain you in my court."

"You mean because I'm black?" Rutherford chuckled. "No, I couldn't stay here. Truth be told, I love my academic life, my studies and my students. And maybe Princess Judith will be able to study as well, to become something more, a more learned person someday."

"The girl *is* very smart," Irv agreed with a nod of his head. "I think she would like to learn things about this history and the big world in the future."

That night Princess Judith arranged the seating so she would be next to Rutherford again, and they were, on more than one occasion, able to hold hands under the table. The California wine flowed and Prince Sol held forth about a Christian fellow he had met who was trying to design a special, very hot oven. Possibly an oven hotter than dragon fire!

"If such a thing was possible," the Merlin challenged, "I would have thought of it by now! Remember who brought this pizza here to our, ah, time."

"Prince Richard of Vaude says he will build such an oven out of clay bricks," Sol announced. He took a sip of his wine and continued. "He'll build a thick brick shell back by our dragon pit, it'll have a sort of cave of bricks beneath, where the fires will burn, and another compartment above, where the temperature will soar and the pizzas can be cooked and then removed to serve with large, long handled wooden spatulas. He thinks he could build it so large that we could make two or three pies at one time."

"And what will happen to Burny then," Judith asked in a surly voice. "He'll be heartbroken if he has nothing to do. He *likes* his job."

"Burny will still be the main attraction, the draw, so to speak, the prince told them, "he'll be okay."

"Yeah," Judith scolded. "What'll he do, just stand there and glower at people all day? What kind of life will that be for a fire-breathing dragon?"

"Burny is a pet," Queen Sophie announced in a haughty tone. "Pets find ways to entertain themselves. Like that big worthless ginger maugy of your father's! Honestly, that cat is *no end* to trouble. Why yesterday he unraveled two of my balls of expensive yarn as I was preparing to do some winter knitting. It took my chambermaid hours to gather all that wool, pull out the knots and re-roll it. And she never found a third ball of bright red that Bird must have hidden in some dark corner."

A ginger head peeked up over the edge of the table from the king's lap at the mention of his name. He snagged a hunk of steak from the edge of Irv's plate and quickly vanished toward the kitchens.

"So Professor," Irv said to change the topic. "As this is your last night of this visit, when will we be seeing you again? Hopefully when you return the snow will be gone from the golf course and we'll be able to play a game or two."

"I know I'll have a week off when the university celebrates Easter if not before," the scholar answered. "Hershel can come and fetch me. I'll be looking forward to your fine hospitality and more of Princess Judith's amazing rhubarb pie as well!"

The king gave his future son-in-law a conspiratorial wink. "We'll have lots to talk about when you return," he said.

That night, Rutherford was awoken by a sound in the hall outside his bed chamber. The door eased open with just the faintest creak and Judith appeared in a long white nightgown with her finger to her lips begging silence. The couple made love as quietly as anyone possibly could and fell asleep in each other's arms. Just before sunrise, Bird pushed the chamber door open with one orange and white striped paw, snuck up onto the bed and butted Judith awake with his head. Rutherford could swear the animal winked a bright yellow eye at him before he turned and followed the princess out.

*Warehouse Castle*

# Part III

# Guess Who's Coming to Dinner?

# 🐉 FORTY-SIX 🐉

"**O**ur daughter, our only daughter, is marrying a svartz? Irving, what are you saying? Have you gone completely geshlagan? This man isn't even Jewish!"

"Doctor Rutherford is studying the Torah. He's going to convert. Well, not exactly convert because he claims he doesn't currently belong to *any* particular faith."

"He's studying with *our* Rabbi?"

"No, he's studying with the Rabbi at a synagogue in Oxford, near where he lives in the future. He tells me they even have a Hebrew studies program at the university and a place for Jewish students called the Oxford Chabad Society."

"Irving, I'm not very happy right now. And where will they live, anyway? Will Judith's husband just show up here when he wants a little slap and a tickle?"

"Judith plans to go back to the future with the good doctor. As a Don at Oxford University, Rutherford has a nice house there on campus. He's assured me that they'll live a very comfortable life."

"So I'm not only gaining a black son-in-law, but I'm losing a daughter, oy!"

"Sophie, darling, think about what Judith's prospects would be if she stayed here. We're the only Hebrew royalty here in this land that we know about. So where would our Judith find a nice Jewish boy that would be her equal socially? Her best hope would be that we marry her off to the son of some Christian king to form a bonding alliance with another kingdom. Would you see our little girl in an arranged marriage? I don't think she'd be happy."

"Oh Irv," his wife cried, "At least I'd get to see her now and then... Alright, I know that sounds selfish. Ach, what can I do?"

"Pray, Sophie," Irv comforted. "We'll just pray that everything will work out for the best and God will do the rest.

As the snow melted away and green shoots appeared from the ground and birdsong began to fill the trees once more, Princess Judith and Queen Sophie had a series of heart-to-heart talks. Judith assured her mother that they would get to visit from time to time.

"Hershel is always tripping back and forth from here to there, mummy."

"Oy, Hershel," the queen replied. "I know he's a good friend to your father but, honestly, I don't like the man."

"From what Roofie says, mum, Hershel's machine goes so quick, you won't have any time for small talk with him." Judith gave her mother a confident nod. "You'll barely climb into his contraption and you'll be there, stepping out again."

"And this future place," the queen nagged, "what's it like? How do you know you'll like it there, tell me that."

"Mummy, you keep saying that. How do I know? I just do!" Judith shrugged her shoulders in frustration. "Rutherford will be there, I love that man, and we'll have lots of California wine...."

"Ach, my daughter the hussy! Drink and men!"

"Mummy," Judith scolded, "you know it's not like that! Roofie has promised me a good life. We'll raise wonderful happy children in a beautiful world full of something Hershel calls 'modern conveniences.' It will be very much like a life of royalty."

As with all their discussions, Sophie ended the meeting with a big, fat, "*I don't know about this!*"

Passover wasn't far behind the green freshness that foretold of spring. The kitchen staff prepared the special kosher diet required by the royal family and the pizza portion of the roadside attraction closed until the holiday had passed. Princess Judith was now counting the days excitedly until her betrothed would magically appear outside the Merlin's dwelling.

In anticipation of the professor's arrival, Judith was busy recruiting her brother to be best man for her wedding. "Easy stuff," the prince told her, "I'm the best man everywhere I go!"

She also asked her friend Deborah and her two sisters to be the bridesmaids. Then the princess painstakingly went over every little detail of what she required for her wedding with the castle staff. She wanted the event to be impressive to Rutherford as well as to all the royalty from the surrounding kingdoms that would be in attendance.

By comparing and reconciling the local calendar with a future calendar from the year 1998, Hershel was able to pinpoint a date for the professor's arrival and thus set a firm date for the ceremony.

The day before Rutherford's predicted arrival Judith was faced with one of the hardest tasks of her young life. Judith realized that before she left for the future she had to say goodbye to her dragon, Burny.

With tears in her pretty eyes, Judith approached Burny's pit at the attraction. She motioned for the giant beast to bring his scaly head down where she could stroke his rough brow.

"Oh, Burny, you poor old thing," she wept. "You do know how much I love you, how I've always loved you!"

The tall beast made an affirmative sound way down in his throat and brought forth his enormous forked tongue to lick her body and face. "Oh Burny," she balled, "this is just so tough for me, but little girls have to grow up one day, do you understand?" The dragon cocked his head to one side and gave her a puzzled look. What was this grow up? Dragons hatched from an egg! Sure, they grew, they grew up and out. What was this crazy human girl saying?

"Oh God, Burny, this is so hard for me to say. I'm a big girl now, a woman. I still love you, I'll always love you and I'll keep you in my heart forever.

"But as a woman, I must say goodbye to the things of my childhood. You've been my best friend, Burny, but I have to leave you now, along with my toys, dolls and plush animals. I need to begin my grown up life and there's no place in it for a dragon. Oh God, Burny, I'm just so sad!"

A deep and pitiful bellow rose from the dragon's throat, and a tear fell from one of his giant yellow eyes, but he nodded that he understood. Burny leaned his long neck down once more, put forth his long, forked tongue and licked Judith's face, then the beast turned, began beating his enormous scaled wings and took off above the trees flying south east toward the sea.

# 🐉 FORTY-SEVEN 🐉

Rutherford's flight arrived right on time to find Queen Sophie and King Irv waiting to whisk him away to the castle. Superstition dictated that the groom should not lay eyes on the bride immediately before the ceremony, but Judith was able to find where they'd hidden her man away and bribed one of the staff to take her to see the professor before they were due on the castle's broad bailey.

"This will only be the first wedding," her lover grinned. "My friends at Oxford have another big do planned for next Sunday. I've told everyone that you're flying in from America, I didn't know how else to explain you. They said we have to have a big wedding at the university. They have lots of gifts to present to us! You'll love my friends, they're just amazing people!"

Princess Judith shot him a quizzical look. A second wedding? They would be married twice? Well, that would certainly cement their nuptial bond! The princess grinned at her betrothed with loving eyes.

"So I'm supposed to be one of these American people now?" Judith asked coyly. "How do Americans speak and act? Should I be studying something about these people before I join you in the future?"

Rutherford gave a hearty laugh. "We have this thing in the future called television. It's a box where you watch people in shows, kinda like watching the theater in Vaude through a small window.

There are Americans on television all the time for you to watch, but I don't think you'll need to try and imitate them. Just be yourself and we'll be fine." Looking at her confusion the man had another thought. "By the way, I have something for you called a passport. It's a small book that proves you came from America…"

"But I didn't really," the princess interrupted. "I'll be coming from here."

"The authorities in my time mustn't know that. They have to have all the proper blanks filled in on their forms."

"Filled in blanks on forms?" the princess asked with even greater puzzlement.

"Too much to explain right now," the professor told her, "just trust me."

"But as I'm not from America, where did I get this passport thingy?" The princess was all in a dither.

"In truth?" Rutherford replied. "I took a photo of you with my cell phone, that's something else I'll explain later because it's too complicated for the moment. I sent it to a cousin of mine who lives in California and he bribed a friend that works for the government to make up a passport for you. It says you're Judith Abrahamson from a place called Rockport, Texas. You may not ever have to show it to anyone, but just in case, we'll be ready."

"And should I be packing my clothes? Won't they look out of place, or do America people dress like we do here in the Wholesale Kingdom?"

Rutherford gave her a reassuring look. "As soon as we arrive, I'm going to take you to a very large store called Marks and Spencer. They have all the most up-to-date styles of dress for you."

"Styles?" the princess's face clouded again. "This future place, England? It's beginning to sound very complicated indeed." The princess mused. "We'll talk about it later, but I'd better go now. My friend Deborah will be knocking at my room anytime to help me into my wedding gown."

The Warehouse Castle was decorated with colorful pennants flying from all the towers and battlements. Over the **portcullis and facing into the courtyard**, the king's men had hung a broad banner embroidered by the queen herself with a single word, **Mahzel**. Guests continued to arrive all through the morning and the queen greeted them each with ale and small breakfast cakes.

Needless to say the wedding went very well, Prince Sol brought some unusual musician friends to perform for the reception. One young lady played a primitive sort of violin, her brother had a hollow wooden tube that he claimed had come all the way from far Afrika. The stick had holes down its length and a single reed attached to the top end that he blew into while covering and uncovering the holes with his fingers. Morrie played his lute while his young nephew pounded out rhythm on various different sized drums.

The reigning monarchs of adjoining kingdoms sat on rows of divans King Irv's servants had hauled out to the courtyard. King Bertram and Queen Alice were there with their six children. Friar Agnello sat with them, commenting on how similar weddings were in his church, except for the fact that no one here mentioned the Savior, Jesus."

King John of Vaude, whom his subjects often referred to as King Four-by-Five behind his back because he was almost as wide as he was tall, took a one full couch with his incredible three-hundred-fifty pound bulk. His queen, Martha had to perch uncomfortably on the arm of that piece of furniture. King John's son, the oven inventor, sat on the lawn to one side with his two beautiful sisters, Princess Anne and Princess Amy.

Smiling beneath damp eyes, King Irv led his only daughter down the aisle to where Professor Rutherford waited with Rabbi Weiss under a white canopy. An aged copy of the Torah sat on the dais before them.

Vows were recited and the party began. Doctor Rutherford and Princess Judith danced the lively steps of the minor-key first dance then a slower, more intimate number. King Irv waited patiently to have a dance of his own with his young daughter who would soon be very absent from his daily life.

As kitchen and other wait staff began loading down the outdoor tables with meats, cheeses and cakes, Princess Judith, now Mrs. R. P. Johnston, went to the stage and had a few brief words with the musicians. The reed player and the violinist nodded their heads rapidly and Judith smiled, turning to face the assembled throng. At a sign from her, the band began a slow minor-key ballad and Judith, her eyes on her new husband began to sing.

"I love you much too much, I've known it from the start,

But then my love is such I can't control my heart,

I love you much too much I ask myself what for,

And darling when we touch, I love you more,

Perhaps I hold your heart too tightly but who am I to say?

If I should hold it lightly, it might slip away,

I love you much too much, you've never really known

I love you oh so much, I'm yours alone"

The fiddler followed the princess's vocal with a long impro-vised solo. When the violin was finished, Judith came back in to sing the song's lyric again, but this time in the original Hebrew.

There followed a long afternoon of dancing, food and drink. Morrie the Jester made some crude jokes about honeymooning cou-ples, virgin brides, and married life drawing loud happy laughter from the diverse and slightly drunk crowd. Judith took her mother aside for one last tearful chat, assuring her that they would see each other again one day.

With the sun touching the tree tops, a noticeably squiffy King Irv excused himself and led his daughter and new son-in-law across the first fairway to the Merlin's cave. A small carpet bag containing some of Judith's personal items had already been loaded into the time machine and someone had tied a few ale cans to the back of the contraption as well as scrawling 'just married' on its tin façade.

Judith hugged her father for a full minute, whispering, "Thanks, pop, thanks for everything. You know how much I love you!" She then backed away, put two fingers beneath her father's jaw and with a tear in her eye said. "Keep your chin up, pop!"

Hershel's machine was not large and he'd never taken more than a single passenger before, so Princess Judith had to duck her head and sit on her husband's knee in order to fit. The machine made a few unusual noises, straining under the increased weight, but finally turned translucent and then disappeared.

# ✦ FORTY-EIGHT ✦

"**H**usband, I feel very sad right now," Queen Sophie announced. "I feel sad, but yet I'm very happy. I miss our Judith, but I understand how happy she is. If only this future England place wasn't so far away!"

The royal couple was seated side-by-side on a divan in the main hall that the staff had hauled back in from the courtyard. Much of the castle's staff was busy cleaning up outside where guests had spilled drinks, dropped food and made a general mess in their celebration. Some of the couches would need to be cleaned before they could be brought back in and there were stacks of dishes and tubs of glasses and tankards also in need of washing.

"I'm just glad it's over," Irv told his wife. "At least Prince Sol is dedicated to his work and doesn't seem to be making any serious pursuit of a mate. I can use a *long* break before we need to go through another wedding."

As if on cue, Prince Sol entered the hall from where he'd been supervising some of the clean-up activities. He plopped himself down in an over-stuffed chair across from his parents, with one leg casually thrown over the chair's arm.

"Hey mom, dad, wasn't that a great wedding? I know I'm gonna miss sis, but she sure got a great send-off." The prince took a nibble from a leftover cake in his hand. "So did you guys notice that red haired daughter of King John's, Amy? Princess Amy of Vaude? I'm thinkin' that if Prince Richard can put in a good word for me, I think I'd like to marry that girl! And it would help bring our king-dom into better relations with Vaude as well, wouldn't it?"

Queen Sophie tried to stifle a giggle as King Irv emitted a groan from deep in his throat. "You're an eligible young man," the queen told her son trying to keep a straight face. "I'm sure there will be plenty of young ladies for you to consider. You don't want to rush into anything."

When the castle was returned to its usual state, the furniture cleaned and the royal dishes stored in the kitchen's vast cupboards, Hershel the Merlin strolled into the main hall where King Irv and Bird were playing with one of the queen's yarn balls.

"Rutherford told me he has a plan to deal with that money stuff, highness. Could you give me a hand? I'm gonna take most of it out of the suitcase and put it in those empty wine boxes that the bottles came in. I'm gonna keep a handful of the stuff for when I travel, but just a very small amount. We can tie the boxes shut with string and have one of your trusted knights put them into my machine. When I get to England, the professor will load them into this transport thing he calls a Ford, bring them to where he lives and then Princess Judith and him will take them to someplace he calls a 'bank' that will store it for them." Hershel looked to still be a little unsure of what he was relaying to his king. "The professor says he'll be putting the money into something called 'accounts,' one in your name and one in Judith's, so you'll have money there if you or Sophie should ever come to visit.

With his daughter gone and his so-called money as well, King Irv passed his days golfing with Hershel, Rabbi Weiss and Friar Agnello. They started making bets on who might get par on this hole or who would emerge with the low score in the game. Father Agnello voiced the opinion that they might be committing some act of sin, but that didn't stop him from laying his money down. After their game, Hershel and King Irv generally had a tankard or two of ale and shared deep philosophical discussions. The Merlin suggested that maybe the king should have Rutherford, the king's son-in-law, write some kind of college paper about how he, King Irv, had invented golf; about how the game was being played in the English Midlands centuries before the Scots introduced golf at St. Andrews.

King Irv gave that consideration, but finally concluded that he was a simple and happy king who didn't want to steal anyone else's thunder. He enjoyed playing this game from the future that gave him exercise and an extra challenge for his days. The kingdom seemed to run along smoothly with only the slightest hint of his hand on the tiller. His knights and his advocates performed all the sweaty, dreary, day-to-day work leaving him with plenty of time to pursue his pastimes. His small portion of this great island seemed immune to battles and strife. All was very well.

That is, it was well until the day Prince Sol came to him with the news that he had succeeded in getting Princess Amy of the House of Vaude in a family way.

"Yup, father, the medic in Vaudeville says she's definitely preggers." The prince told him with a taciturn nod of his head.

King Irv invited Good King John of Vaude to play a game of golf so they might talk. King John, all three-hundred-and-some pounds of him, showed up at Warehouse Castle the next morning in a sedan chair borne on the shoulders of six poor souls from his laboring class. Irv had custom golf clubs fashioned as a gift to his fellow monarch, although his neighbor's girth made swinging the clubs difficult. As they approached the first tee, Irv noticed that his opponent sat in his conveyance constantly gnawing on a large leg of cold lamb. When the man gripped his driver to address his ball, the grease from the lamb made it difficult to maintain his hold on the club.

"I'm not fond of this game!" King John proclaimed. "It's just *too much* bloody work. Do you play chess, highness? Now there's a game I enjoy! I can remain seated on my throne with food and drink at my fingertips and not have to move anything but my one hand!"

King Irv told him that, yes, he played chess, but preferred to be outdoors with the sunshine and birdsong. The fat monarch shot him a bewildered look, as though he, Irv, must be some kind of idiot. "Outdoors," King John scoffed down his nose, "is for lower classes that have no one to wait on them!"

They did manage to discuss plans for Prince Sol to wed Princess Amy and seal a bond of mutual defense and other benefits for their two kingdoms, but Irv had to endure endless complaints about the inconvenience of King John's having to constantly climb in and out of his sedan chair every time he was required to hit his golf ball. The man didn't seem cognizant of King Irv's walking an entire seven existing holes two and a half times while toting a full bag of clubs on his shoulder.

To Irv's satisfaction, King John agreed that he would host and pay for the affair. Only maybe Irv could provide some of that wonderful sweet Dragon Piss wine for the celebration. King Irv choked back a grin. I feel very sorry for my son, Irv thought. But then again, maybe he can be the positive force to turn King Vaude's lazy king-dom around.

"So where's your princess these days?" the obese monarch in-quired of him. "Very black skinned chap he seemed, that husband of hers, not from around here I don't think."

Remembering some of the coaching his son-in-law had given him, Irv replied. "Leon, they went back to Leon. That's across the water on the continent near Italia."

"Lots of Moors there," King John remarked scornfully. "Lazy black Moors!"

King Irv bit his tongue and didn't answer.

"We can have a chess match, you and me, at my daughter's wedding," King John stated, his grin lifting two of his many chins skyward. "Now that will be a fun challenge!"

# FORTY-NINE

King Irv learned that, soon after Judith's marriage to Dr. Rutherford, Prince Richard of Vaude had brought his little sister Amy to the roadside attraction to sell the pizza cooked in his new hotter oven as Prince Sol had asked him to do. The Jewish prince had required Amy to work late, helping him straighten up at the end of the day. That was how he had been able to seduce the girl.

But no matter now, what was done was done and the two were scheduled to be married on the mid-summer solstice. King John had sent Friar Agnello around to school Prince Sol in the Catholic faith, telling him that any children they bore had to be raised in the Church of Rome or he, Prince Sol, would burn in hell forever. When the prince replied that he didn't believe in Jesus or the Church of Rome, Friar Agnello shrugged his narrow shoulders and told him, "If you don't believe, the Church has no hold over you, my son. Maybe you could join your father and me in a round of golf sometime?" he smiled.

As the wedding plans progressed, Sol and Amy were busy turning the café at the roadside attraction into the world's first true Pizza Parlor. They hired a pupil of Morrie's' who was getting good on the lute to sing bawdy songs while the tourists dined. They also installed torches high on the walls so they could remain open later into the night and hired staff to work extra hours, so they would have some free time to cuddle in the prince's office.

Profits were soaring, which made King Irv so happy that he

offered to share some of this wealth with King John. King John simply scoffed at the offer. "Pizza," he spat in a disgusted tone. "These lowly proles will eat anything! A real man requires meat, *Meat*! And plenty of it," he shouted as he gnawed on his customary joint of lamb.

Irv and Sophie grew nervous as the solstice approached. Did the Wholesale Kingdom really need to be affiliated with such a lazy monarch as King John? When Irv had asked how the man could lead his knights into battle, should the need arise, John had simply told him that his knights were quite capable of handling any situation. "I keep them on their toes by keeping them deprived and hungry," the obese monarch had told him. "If they win the battle, they know they'll be well fed afterwards. If they lose? Well, then I haven't wasted a lot of resources on them, have I? And I can always have my loyal servants carry me into the thick of it in my chair," he chuckled, "if it should come to that. But of course, it never will."

Irv and Sophie agreed that they hoped the apple wouldn't fall too close to the tree. They prayed daily that Princess Amy would prove a good and obedient wife for their son and not end up a lazy lout like her father. But in the end, what could they do beyond pray and trust their son's judgment? When Prince Sol brought her around to dinner, the girl seemed to be intelligent. The friars at the church in Berten-on-Cherwell had educated her, giving her some skills in mathematics and the language even if her learning was mixed with a load of Christian superstition.

The solstice, and the prince's wedding day, arrived all too soon. Irv and Sophie saddled up their finest horses for the ride east to Castle Vaude in the company of the Wholesale Kingdom's twelve noble and true knights. Irv and his men wore the summer weight armor John the Smith had made them a few years before, his queen a long gown of sky blue with a large Star of David embroidered across it in blinding gold thread. "It's something Judith calls 'Bling'," Sophie told him. As the wedding was held on a Saturday, all the knights word blue yarmulké on their heads. Irv had his under his regal crown.

They arrived to find that King John was ensconced in the south tower, overlooking a bailey that featured a stone surface laid in a checkered pattern, white stone alternating with black slate. Tables, chairs and colorful banners were laid out beyond the broad bailey on a lawn that stretched down toward the river. Above the fat monarch on the south tower, a large banner bearing the crest of Vaude fluttered in the breeze. Looking up, Irv noticed that a white flag bearing a blue Star-of-David waved above the opposite northern tower.

King John lifted a long megaphone tube to his face hollering down, "I thought we might have that game of Chess before our children take their vows."

"You want to come down and sit somewhere at a table for a game?" Irv shouted up cupping his hands in front of his face.

"Come down?" came the amplified reply. "I'm not coming down. Too much effort as I've already been carried up to this height. You climb the stairs to the opposing tower. I'll have my vassals, dressed in both white and black, line up on the large board of my courtyard. You can easily see that they are dressed as knights, bishops, pawns and such. My queen will play herself and my young son will assume my place as king. I've assigned some of my more noble subjects to play your good queen and yourself. So get up to your tower, man! The game is about to begin! You will shout down your opening move. There's a megaphone by your chair in the north tower along with meat and ale to sustain you. Now scramble up there and let's allow the game to start! The sooner I defeat you, the sooner the wedding may begin!"

And defeat King Irv he did! Irv was too anxious to pay the requisite attention to the game, not to mention distracted by all the shouting down to living chess pieces. He got off a good opening gambit, but soon found himself in check time and time again. He kept hearing King John's hearty laughter as it flew forth around the fat stick of meat stuck in his face. King Irv never even touched the joint of meat beside his own chair. This is not the proper way to play a thoughtful game like chess, he told himself.

When the chess match had finished it took half of an hour for King John's men to ease him down the circular staircase to the festivities. There was already plenty of food and drink to be had around the grounds of Vaude Castle, but also lots of questions. Would the obese king be able to walk his daughter down the aisle? Queen Martha insisted that he would, that he must! While they waited, the guests consumed tankard after tankard of the monarch's ale. Few showed any interest in the Dragon Piss Wine that was being offered all around by the castle's wait staff.

The large king finally came through the door of the south tower, but so out-of-breath that he had to sit for another long stretch of minutes while some of his helpers fanned him with giant wooden paddles and the remainder wiped sweat from his face and body with a pile of thick towels. As he recovered from his descent from the tower, Princess Amy stood beside him tapping her foot and eyeing daggers his way. "Daddy," she repeated over and over in a loud whisper, "why do you have to spoil my special day for me?"

King John finally managed to get to his feet under the scornful eye of Queen Martha. He extended his elbow to Princess Amy with a loud, embarrassing burp. They started down the aisle toward the altar, but had to stop and rest every four or five paces. A retainer walked beside them, extending a hunk of half-raw meat before his majesty at each stop so the king might keep up his strength.

By the time the princess and her father reached where Friar Agnello stood, the audience was becoming bored and restless. The good padre was considering abbreviating the vows to finish before fist fights broke out among the assembled guests. Irv and Sophie waited patiently, silently praying for their poor son Prince Sol.

Giovanni Agnello read some passages from the New Testament in his broken English, trying to gauge the crowd and what they might endure. At the sound of increasing angry mumbles, he moved straight to the vows, softly mumbling, "You are a rude pig," at King John under his breath. If the four-by-five monarch heard, he showed no sign of it. He simple twitched and eyed his joint of meat only a few feet away in his butler's hands.

Once the good friar pronounced the prince and princess man and wife, a cheer went up from the crowd and drunken onlookers joined the happy couple in dancing. Queen Martha announced that the king would dance a number with his daughter, but King John only lasted a dozen steps of the Terpsichore before he gave a loud, hungry moan and collapsed on the grass with his eyes rolling heavenward. His butler held a cold lamb leg down to the monarch who hungrily ripped flesh from the bone with a look of ecstasy.

Guests headed for the exits shortly thereafter. The king's antics

Skoot Larson

had just been too much for them, even with the prospect of more food and drink. King Irv's knights gave him sorry looks, although no one had the courage to offer apologies for King John's abominable performance. The fat king had fallen asleep across one of the tables, squashing a dozen or more of the wedding cakes there-on.

## FIFTY

Prince Sol and his bride moved into an unused suite of rooms in Warehouse Castle. Princess Anne requested that King Irv might grant her a room as well. She said she wanted to be close to her big sister, but Queen Sophie surmised that it was more about distancing herself from her rather gross father.

Prince Sol appointed an assistant manager at the roadside attraction, to whom he delegated increasing responsibility as the man learned the ropes. His chosen helper was the son of King Irv's noble knight, Sir Jakob. Jakob Junior was a conscientious helper and welcomed increasing responsibility, so Prince Sol now had the time to play more golf with his father, their Merlin and the Rabbi.

The prince was also teaching his new brother-in-law, Prince Richard, how to play golf. Unlike his father, Richard enjoyed being outdoors. He was an avid bird watcher and a skilled horseman. If the day ever came, Sol and Richard both agreed that Prince Richard would be very capable of leading the Castle Vaude army into battle. He was everything his father was not, having broad shoulders, long legs and a narrow waist, as well as strong wrists that made him a skilled ambidextrous swordsman.

The golf course now boasted a full nine holes. Irv and Hershel had a standing game with the king's son and son-in-law every Tuesday and Friday morning. Days when Prince Sol's presence wasn't required at the attraction, the two young men would enjoy a few ales with their elders, discussing the philosophy of governing and the responsibility a monarchy owed to its subjects. Irv was impressed by the understanding the two young princes displayed. Confidence in his own young son increased daily although the king was still bothered by what his son-in-law Rutherford had told him about no graves being found for his family in the future. It nagged at his mind that Prince Sol might not live to rule his kingdom.

Then came the Friday morning when Prince Richard showed up late for their scheduled match. The young man appeared a little shaken, but still firmly in control of himself. "Father died yesterday," he announced to his golfing partners. "It really wasn't any surprise, the way the man lived."

"Oh, I'm so sorry for you," King Irv told him.

"Don't be," the young prince replied tersely. "While I loved my father, he was a tyrant and a glutton. Our kingdom will, I'm sorry to say, be much better off without him."

Prince Richard then addressed his ball and, with a number three wood, wacked his ball straight down the center of the first fairway. When putting was completed on that first green, the young man spoke again. "I hope you will all be in attendance at my coronation next Sunday."

The air around him was thick with questions. Finally Hershel blurted out, "So what the hell happened, anyway?"

"The King was on maneuvers with his knights," Richard told them. "They were out in that wild area far to the east of any of our villages when a bear came out of a thick stand of trees. Father's knights had no trouble subduing the animal, but apparently when father had seen the creature lumbering out of the woods in the direction of his sedan chair, I'm told that he turned white as a ghost, clutching at his chest. His knights say he dropped the lamb leg he'd been eating and fell out of his conveyance landing on his head. His quaking bearers weren't sure what to do, but one of the men in the back of father's chair started shouting, "The King is down! Some-one render aid to our king!"

Sir Markus, King John's lead knight, turned from the bear. Spy-ing his king face down in the tall grass, he ran to the monarch's side only to pronounce the man dead. I'm told that he listened with an ear to our ruler's chest, put two finger's to the man's neck seeking a pulse, then raised those fingers up to close our late king's eyes. Sir Markus shouted to his men, "The king is dead. Long live the king! So can I get some help to lift King John's carcass back into his chair that we may carry him home to Vaude Castle?"

Although soon-to-be King Richard wasn't so upset about his father's demise, the news put a damper on the day's round of golf. Much of the game was played in a heavy silence. King Irv finished three shots under par, but it didn't make him feel any better. He returned to his throne to show his cat, Bird, a lot of affection as he pondered his own mortality.

# FIFTY-ONE

King Richard's coronation was day to night from his sister's wedding only months before. King Irv and his knights once again came fully kitted out in summer weight armor and the queen wore her sky blue frock. The event also, conveniently, served as King John's funeral although no one had much positive to say about him or his rule. Newly crowned King Richard, as his first regal act, called forth the six poor souls who had spent many years carrying his father's bloated body in that infernal sedan chair.

"For your service, above and beyond the call of duty," he loudly intoned from the raised stage that held his throne, "I wish to grant each of you and your families a plot of land, six hectares square where you may farm for yourselves. You will each have a newly thatched cottage built there-on by my knights in which you may live undisturbed on your new land. You are here-by released from any further service to the crown beyond the percentage of the crops you grow that may be levied in taxes. I pray that you each and every one enjoy your well-earned retirement."

A murmur arose from the crowd. This new king seemed to be a good man who cared about his people!

"I do further declare that each and every one of my knights will receive a regular ration of meat, fruit and vegetables each day, so they may go strong into any conflict and keep themselves always at the ready to stand with me and defend our land!"

At this declaration, the assembled knights of Vaude Kingdom sent up a loud, raucous cheer and were joined by King Irv's knights.

"We are all your most loyal servants, King Richard," lead knight Markus shouted. His men behind him began chanting, "Long live the King, long live good King Richard!"

At the next Tuesday's golf game, newly crowned King Richard turned up in casual attire to play golf with Prince Sol, Friar Agnello and Irv. "I need to do a lot to make amends for the way my late father ruled," he told his friends. "The more I dig into his affairs, the more embarrassed I feel."

"You can't be held responsible for your father's mistakes," Prince Sol remarked.

"But I must accept such responsibility," King Richard breathed. "I must if I am to win the trust of my people... Our people, majesty," he said looking King Irv straight in the eye.

"Father mismanaged our affairs of state. His only concern was feeding himself, both his enormous gut and his even larger ego! He wasn't truly interested in our subjects or how they fared. His *primary* thoughts were about food and food only."

"So many times in the chapel in Vaudeville, I preached about the sin of gluttony," the good friar shook his head. "I don't think he ever heard my sermons. Imagine, his highness actually was so rude as to carry large pieces of meat into my church. The entire congregation could hear him slurping and loudly masticating that lamb all through my service! And, of course, he was too large to get down on his knees to pray without three or four of his retainers there to lift him up again."

"Well, from this day forth," King Richard pledged, "my kingdom will stand in alliance with the Wholesale Kingdom." Shifting his gaze toward King Irv, he said, "We share a very long border, as I'm sure your highness is aware, stretching from the House of Hamp in the north clear to Berks' Kingdom in the south. Our lands are further united by my sister's marriage to our good Prince Sol here. I pray that the noble knights of our two kingdoms may stand together, side-by-side, in defense of both our lands. We may profess differing faiths, but so much more do we have in common, if you are in agreement, your highness?"

# 🐉 FIFTY-TWO 🐉

lthough neither kingdom was faced with an outside threat, this new alliance appeared to work very well. Matters of state concerning both of the realms were discussed regularly Tuesdays and Fridays on the golf course. When one kingdom was short of some item, say wheat grain, the other would do all they could to assist. Holiday festivals, both Jewish and Christian, were jointly celebrated and enjoyed. The subjects of each realm became more aware and sympathetic of their neighbors traditions and beliefs.

Queen Sophie, in spite of this new era of peace and understanding, missed her daughter unbearably. She was constantly kvetching at her husband as she secretly blamed him for allowing their daughter to marry some foreigner and leave. Irv had a number of consultations with his Merlin, who still made occasional trips to the future to play golf with the professor. It was finally agreed between Hershel, Rutherford and Irv that Queen Sophie would make a trip to the future. Princess Judith sent modern clothes from Marks and Spencer in her mother's size. Sophie complained that these new clothes didn't feel right, but she wore them anyway when she appeared at the Merlin's cave to mount the time machine and make a trip to see her daughter.

Queen Sophie arrived in the parking lot of the Castle Golf Club to find her daughter and Professor Rutherford Johnston waiting in front of a shiny black lump-shaped thing on wheels. Her daughter was barely recognizable in her modern white pant suit outfit.

The former Princess opened a door in the wheeled thing and handed her mother into a very comfortable leather seat, so soft that the
queen sunk down an inch or two into it. Her son-in-law got into the
machine in front of her on one side while Judith entered through
a door on the other. Rutherford twisted something beside a thin
inner wheel and there came a roaring sound from the front of the
contraption. The man put his hand on a short stick between himself
and her daughter and the black shape began to move forward at a
fast clip. Queen Sophie was terrified, not knowing what to think,
but she noticed that her daughter and son-in-law seemed comfortable with this, so she relaxed herself and watched the green grass,
trees and hedges that rolled by outside her window in this weird
black carriage.

They stopped beside a brick building, not exactly a castle, but
not a peasant style hovel either. "This is home," Judith told her
mother, Wait 'till you see how nice it is inside."

Climbing from the black conveyance, Queen Sophie noted that
there was a chill in the air, but upon entering her daughter's house
it was toasty and warm. She glanced around but could see no fireplace. Warm air seemed to blow from a grate high up on the wall.

The queen's feet sunk into a thick beige carpet that extended
from one wall to the next and even into the next room and up a long
staircase. The queen kicked off her shoes to feel the soft floor covering with her toes. There were no bare stones visible on the walls.
They appeared to be covered with a pale, velvety material. She ran
her hand over the wallpaper emitting a soft "oh!" as she did. The
far wall was hidden behind floor-to-ceiling shelves full of books.
On one center shelf, she noticed a window in which she could see
two people seated behind a desk talking.

"You home is beautiful!" Queen Sophie told her daughter in a soft voice filled with awe. "Are those painted pictures in the frames over there? Those ships look so lifelike! And those smaller frames on the tabletop, are those pictures of you with that little girl? They are even more real looking."

Judith laughed. "Those are something we call photographs, mummy. They *are* real pictures of me and Tiffany."

At the mention of her name, a chubby, milk chocolate-skinned bomb with her mother's curly blond hair came sailing down the stairs and into the room. "Gramma Sophie?" she inquired, then jumped up on an overstuffed chair with her arms out for as hug. The queen took a step forward and wrapped her arms around the small girl. "I love you, gramma," squealed the four-year-old. "How come nobody could every show me photographs of you? Daddy has lots of photos of my other gramma."

"Tiffany, darling, you shouldn't stand on the furniture," Rutherford scolded with a chuckle. "Why don't you take Gramma Sophie upstairs and show her your room while mummy and I open some California wine for her?"

The excited child grabbed Sophie's hand and pulled her towards the stairs shouting, "Come on, gramma. I'll introduce you to Winnie the Pooh! He's my bear."

When Queen Sophie and Tiffany came back down the stairs, her son-in-law had wine waiting for her in one of those modern goblet glasses. They dined on braised chicken, mashed potatoes with gravy, lightly steamed asparagus and apple pie. "Chicken is my very favorite," young Tiffany giggled. "I'm so glad I finally got to meet you gramma," the child said, rubbing her head against the queen's arm.

When Judith showed the queen to her room, Sophie was a little surprised. The bed seemed very small and had no canopy over it. The former princess noticed her mother's questioning look. "It's called a 'queen-sized' bed," Judith told her. "It will be plenty big enough for you to sleep comfortably. And we don't need a cover over our beds here because we don't have birds or bats in the house. All our windows are sealed with glass."

"But in the summer, don't you need to remove the glass so a breeze can cool the rooms?"

Her daughter laughed again. "We have a machine called an 'air conditioner' that blows cold air into all the rooms without our having to open any windows."

As Judith mentioned windows, Queen Sophie walked over to the one in her room. "There are other houses exactly like your outside, daughter. Is this a village to some king's castle?"

"This is the university campus mummy, the higher learning school. The houses you see are for the other professors like Roofie. Across the road are the buildings where people go to classes." She smiled, "I'm taking classes here myself. I'm studying our English language so some day I might be able to teach like Roofie does."

"And the local king?" her mother inquired.

"We have no local king, mummy. The entire island is ruled by one monarch, Queen Elizabeth."

"A queen rules? What about her husband? Should not a man rule as king?"

Judith laughed again. Our queen has been on the throne of England for nearly fifty years. From all I've learned, she has always been a very good ruler. Maybe we can take a drive down to London tomorrow and you can see her castle, Buckingham Palace."

# 🐉 FIFTY-THREE 🐉

Over the week of her visit, Queen Sophie learned all about modern times. She watched as her son-in-law took pictures of her and her granddaughter, Tiffany, with something he called his cell phone. She noted that the frozen images were immediately visible through a small window on the back of the small instrument, and later Rutherford brought the images forth from something he called his computer on a sheet of paper.

She also enjoyed watching some very funny shows on that window thing they called a television, though she was still mystified as to how those people's pictures were able to move in that small box. She learned that the thing they rode in was called a motor car. The particular one her daughter and son-in-law owned was also known as a Ford Granada.

But most of all, Sophie enjoyed her granddaughter. They played together in a park where there were swings, monkey bars and a big quickly spinning disc thing that Tiffany called a merry-go-round. They walked along the River Thames together and one afternoon even rented a small boat to row and float on the water.

Sophie's children took them to a place called Milton Keynes where there were large and small shops. Some of the places of business were almost as large as Warehouse Castle inside. Tiffany dragged her to a favorite toy store, where Sophie bought the girl two large dolls and a hobby horse. At John Lewis, a business her daughter referred to as a 'department store,' she bought Tiffany a number of outfits of clothing along with some tops and hats for herself. Seeing the ecstasy on her small granddaughter's face, the queen smiled and silently thanked Hershel the Merlin for all those funny pound note papers he had given to her to spend in this future time.

Queen Sophie discovered a public house close to her daughter's home where she could sip an ale and have lunch with Tiffany. The young girl suggested they eat something called 'fish and chips' which was served with mashed green peas the child called 'mushy peas.' Sophie found this fish and chips dish quite to her liking and told herself that Irv would probably like it as well. Maybe the king would return here with her one day. Her heart ached to share this wonderful grandchild with her husband.

The week went by all too fast and soon they were driving back to the golf club where the Merlin would meet them in his machine. Tiffany insisted on accompanying her new fav gramma to Hershel's time thingy. They sat on the porch of the golf club bar waiting for the time machine to materialize. Sophie sipped a final California wine while Tiffany drank something she called a Coke and Sophie's children each downed a pint glass of Mann's Strong Ale.

Back at Warehouse Castle, Queen Sophie tried to tell her husband about all the amazing miracle things she had witnessed in the future. She showed her husband the photographs Rutherford had printed for her out of his computer. King Irv marveled at the beautiful granddaughter they shared somewhere in the future and the fine house his princess daughter now occupied, but showed little interest in traveling through time in Hershel's contraption.

Queen Sophie summoned Hershel to her quarters where she begged him to find some better way she could share their lovely grandchild with stubborn old Irving. The Merlin said he would look into it, but made no promises. "I got some ideas," he told her, "but I don't want to raise your hopes before I check things out."

It was ten or twelve days later that Hershel's machine materialized in the pasture and the Merlin ran excitedly toward the castle's back door. Under his arm he carried a flat black square. It looked a bit like her son-in-law's cell phone thing, only about three times larger. In his hand, he held that funny framed crystal thing like that which powered his time machine. He shouted for Wendy, the downstairs maid, asking her to please fetch the queen to his presence.

Hershel set the crystal thing down on the table, aimed directly up toward the sun, then folded open the other flat, black box. He twisted some wires that connected his sun panel to the cell phone like box. When Queen Sophie appeared, he nodded toward the screen where Sophie's granddaughter danced in a field of flowers.

"Oh," the queen shouted, fanning herself with both her hands then, "Irving," she shouted. "Irving, come quick! Hershel has brought pictures of our little Tiffany, moving pictures!"

The king was by her side in a heartbeat. "This is Judith's little girl?" he queried. "Oh my, she is beautiful! She looks like me with a darker tone to her skin!"

The proffered video was in vibrant full color. The child danced around the playground near Oxford where Sophie and she had spent so many happy hours. Then the scene changed and Princess Judith's voice came from the flat box. "Hello mummy, daddy! We figured out how to share some of our happiness with you. Hershel says he can bring you these moving pictures of us from time to time on a small disc so you can watch Tiffany grow up. He also says he's working on something where he can take pictures of you that we can watch here!"

"Is this some kind of witchcraft?" Irv asked his Merlin. "How can we see these moving pictures?"

"Hey," Hershel told him. "It's something that's all over the future. They call it television, majesty."

"I've seen this," Queen Sophie told Irv, nodding her head rapidly. "I saw some very funny people on this television. Believe me, it's a real thing… in the future. I guess here now as well. I love these moving pictures of our Tiffany!"

"Well, I'm glad if this makes you happy," Irv told her. "Our granddaughter is a very pretty child!"

# FIFTY-FOUR

The years passed. Irv never got up the courage to travel to the future for a visit to his daughter and son-in-law. Hershel often brought back video discs of the future family and he filmed Sophie and Irv to bring their images to Rutherford, Judith and Tiffany.

King Irv played golf almost every day. He left much of the kingdom's business to Prince Sol who had such a good feel for what needed to be done. Along with his brother-in-law, King Richard, Sol was able to make great strides in ruling fair and equitably. Hershel continued to bring new ideas to make life easier. To better care for the golf course, the Merlin brought a grass cutting machine from the future. It worked when hooked up to one of Hershel's quartz sun panels. The gardener's men pushed it over the fairways, a sun panel strapped on top of their heads, and the cut grass flew from beneath it, leaving everything nice and trim. To manicure the greens, they simply turned a knob that lowered the blades and cut the fescue shorter.

Hershel's sun panels also turned fan blades that blew cool air into the castle windows in the heat of summer. He also brought something he called 'electric fire' that could produce heat in the hearth without the burning of wood, but it didn't catch on. People were very suspicious of fire that didn't burn anything. It seemed too much like some kind of Biblical prophecy.

Queen Sophie made regular trips to visit her daughter and granddaughter every year. Each time, she returned in an excited state with more news about how Tiffany was growing. She also reported that their daughter, Judith, had done very well in this university school and now was something they called a Master of English Literature. "Our daughter," she told her husband, "is writing books. Books that they call best sellers, because they are so popular! She tells the story of kings, queens and knights just like us, but she calls them 'fantasy' tales. Judith has also written a story for children about a dragon that cooks pizza and people are buying it all over someplace she calls the 'world!' She's even selling it in that California place where they make that excellent wine!"

"I'm proud of her and happy for her," King Irv answered smugly stroking Bird. The orange cat had become a little on the heavy side and his muzzle was turning more white than ginger.

"Irving, you dolt," his queen hollered staring down at him with her hands on her hips, "*She* is making a fortune! Judith is bringing in more money than all that stuff Hershel found in that suitcase so many years ago. And Rutherford has done something he calls 'investing' with our paper pounds. He says that if we were ever to move to the future, we'd be almost as rich as their powerful modern queen!"

Irv set his tankard down and stared at his wife and queen. "How could this be?" he asked her. Bird stirred in irritation.

"I don't know and I don't care, husband. But I think I'd like to live in this future England place. I'd like to have a house with deep carpet and velvet walls... And be close to our daughter and granddaughter."

"Well, it's something to think about," King Irv remarked.

And that's how life went on, day by day. Queen Sophie kvetched about moving to the future and King Irv played golf, drank ale, pampered his ginger maugy and delegated the running of the Wholesale Kingdom to his son.

They often had video discs from Judith and Rutherford in which they enjoyed watching the antics of their little Tiffany. And as the discs continued, their granddaughter grew taller in each one until she was a buxom young woman with an Oxford scholar boyfriend by her side. Where had the time gone Irv suddenly asked himself?

Then came the day when Prince Sol and King Richard announced on the golf course that they had attended a conference outside Londres with many other monarchs from the island. Some of these kings said that they'd heard frightful tales from the northern borders. There had been threats from the lands to the north and even from lands across the sea. If their island was to survive, they needed to form an alliance that united all the tiny kingdoms together into one large entity. At the least, they needed some kind of mutual defense agreement.

Prince Sol had proposed that they put their individual kingdoms under the leadership of one man, a sort of super king. The assembled monarchs had voted and chosen King Richard of Vaude to represent them. Richard quickly proclaimed Sol to be one of his Earls, The Earl of Wholesale, and stated that the prince would have a strong voice in the formation of this new larger kingdom.

"They have chosen to call the new land Ænglande." Sol told his father.

Skoot Larson

"You mean England?" the king asked with a puzzled face remembering the history his son-in-law Rutherford had relayed to him. "No, it will be Ænglande!" his son told him with surety. "We wish to seek our own special identity. We must do away with things Roman or from other cultures; even what you believe may be our own future. Our new king has promised tolerance for all the differing beliefs of our subjects. As you know, Father Agnello is good friends with our Rabbi…"

"*Father* Agnello? Do you mean the good Friar?"

"*Friar* sounds awfully Roman." His son intoned, eyes toward the ceiling. "It's an *Italian* word, is it not? And I believe it means 'father' in that language, so all the priests of Ænglande from this day forth, even the many who actually *are* Roman will be addressed as 'father.' We feel it is what we must do! And those priests that attended our conference have all pledged tolerance for the Jews of our island nation and the heathens as well."

King Irv was bothered by this latest news his son had brought. He had always enjoyed his role as king and the respect he received from the people of his kingdom. He also liked being able to play golf and drink ale as he pleased without having to do much work in the sweaty, dreary sense.

After the game finished Irv strolled across the fairway to call on his Merlin. "Hershel, old friend," the king spoke as the Merlin popped open two cans of ale and handed one to him, "Everything seems to be changing these days. Prince Sol has just told me there's a plan afoot to unite all the surrounding kingdoms into one." Irv continued, relaying all of what his son and King Richard had told him. "Imagine, calling us all Ænglande!" Irv took a long pull from his ale can then rolled thoughtful eyes skyward. "Maybe it is time for me to go to the future. Sophie says I have a lot of money there. Although I wouldn't be looked up to as a monarch, she says I could pretty much live the same life that I love there, playing golf, enjoying the company of my cat, drinking ale and, as an added bonus, I'd be reunited with my darling Judith and meet my grandchild, Tiffany. How many years has it been since I held my girl in my arms? Likely as not, I won't be king here much longer anyway if all the lands unite, maybe it's time for me to retire and live in the future."

"I know Sophie's been thinking you should do this for some time, Irv," Hershel told him reaching around for a fresh ale. She's got her eye on an overpriced place they call a 'condo,' It's like a private apartment in a castle-like structure right on the golf course. Your front windows would look out over the eighth green and the old 'chapel.' You couldn't beat that!"

"And you, Hershel, would you also buy one of these condos?"

"No, I don't think so," the Merlin replied with sad eyes. "When I bring you to the future, I'll have to say goodbye, old buddy."

King Irv's eye widened in surprise. "But why? I always hoped that if I made this move you would be staying on with us in the future?"

"Irv, this isn't easy for me, but I'll be making only one trip back to Warehouse Castle. And you better decide to make your move pretty soon." A tear formed in the corner of Hershel's eye. "Irv, I'm dying and I want to die in this familiar cave that's always been my home. This National Health doctor in the future? He tells me I've got something he calls cancer growing inside 'a me and it's eating me up. I saw some of the people there at the hospital that they're supposed to be *curing* of this disease and they all look worse than I feel. Their hair is falling out and they get sick when they eat. I don't wanna live like that! I'll bring you, Sophie and Bird to England then I'm gonna come back here and, if I have the strength, play some golf with the Rabbi and talk to him about my life and what might lay beyond. I mean I think I've lived a good life here…"

"But how did you get this cancer thing living inside you?" Irv asked with concern written all over his face.

"The medic said something about exposure… exposure to lead and radiation, I don't know. Myself, I think it might be just too much travelin' through time."

"Traveling through time? Oy, God! Do you think Judith, Sophie, even Rutherford might get this cancer thing?" Hershel gave a hollow laugh. "Irv, my friend, me and the Rabbi, we're some years older than you. We've lived long and full lives. We were around Warehouse Castle when your father, King Dave was alive. You're still a young man. Besides, I've been bouncing back and forth through time maybe thirty, forty times a year over the last decade. The rest of you haven't been in my time machine, what, maybe a dozen rides in all that time? No, Irv, I think you are safe enough."

King Irv stood, stepped forward and threw his arms around Hershel, tears flowing freely. "My God I'm going to miss you, old friend!" The two men remained in a tight bear hug for a full minute. When they broke off Irv said, "I'll go tell Sophie to pack whatever we might need. I'll say goodbye to Sol and we'll be ready to go whenever you're ready."

Bird eyed the cat carrier that Judith had sent from the future skeptically. If they thought he was getting into *that* confining space, they were crazier then he believed most humans were anyway. He paced back and forth across the bailey as Irv and Judith carried their small carpetbag of mementos from the castle and summoned aides to ferry their kit to the Merlin's cave.

"So you don't want to come with me?" Irv asked Bird as the ginger maugy wound around his ankles. "Do you remember my girl Judith? We're going to be reunited with her." Bird gave this some thought, but still knew he shouldn't appear too eager. Finally, he let Queen Sophie give him a shove into the plastic and steel carton. As Irv lifted Bird's carrier into the time machine, he could swear he heard the ginger cat purring.

# 🐉 EPILOGUE 🐉

King Irv, now known as Irving Abrahamson-Smyth, arrived in the future just in time for his granddaughter Tiffany's high school graduation. The girl had taken 'O' levels in English language as well as Mathematics. Tiffany set aside lots of time to get to know the grandfather she had never met face-to-face. To Irv's surprise, his granddaughter played golf and was quite skilled at the game!

Irv also became reacquainted with his dear daughter Judith, who now preferred to be addressed simply as 'Judy.' "Judy and Roofie" was how she introduced herself and her scholarly husband wherever they went. She still possessed the power to melt his old heart when she addressed him as 'pop,' bringing back a flood of memories from when she was a small waif of a girl toting home bunnies and salamanders from around the castle grounds.

Bird also remembered Judith, but quickly struck up a love affair with Tiffany. When the granddaughter came to visit, Bird made a beeline for the young woman demanding attention and affection. Tiffany was happy to oblige the old tom.

Irv and Sophie were very comfortable in their three bedroom condominium overlooking the Castle Golf Club course. Irv had no interest in driving one of those 'car' things although he bought something called a 'Lexus' for Sophie when she obtained her driving license. Tiffany drove a small bright red car called a Fiesta and often came to pick Irv up and drive him to her favorite pub in Oxford for fish and chips along with an ale or two.

Bird quickly learned all the neat hiding places in their new digs. The ginger tom had a cat flap in the rear entrance, but he was always waiting to welcome his master at the door when Irv returned home.

The former King Irv was playing a round of golf with two of Rutherford's Oxford colleagues one fine and clement morning a few months later. Both the scholars enjoyed sharing a foursome with this strange man that told such fascinating stories about ancient England, almost as though he'd been there and lived through it.

Irv's game was going quite well until they started the back nine, which ran down the other side of his old castle's ruins. Off the tenth tee, which had recently been changed from its original location that Irv was used to back home, he hooked his ball badly into a thick stand of larch trees. The old former king had no idea how his ball had made its way into such a thicket. And worse still, he hadn't a clue how he would be able to knock it out without losing ground. He could hear the others laughing as they strolled down the fairway past him. In utter frustration, Irv took his nine iron, deciding he'd simply smack the ball so hard and fast that it would fly through the treetops and find a spot closer to the green.

More laughter from the dog-leg leading to the green told him that his shot had not gone well. Stepping out of the copse of trees, he couldn't immediately locate his ball. Rutherford and his pals were already on the short turf surrounding the hole. Irv strolled slowly across the wide lawn leading toward the ninth hole. From halfway across, he noticed his ball. It sat neatly in the center of a deep depression filled with sand. He knew this didn't baud well for the ten pounds he'd bet his son-in-law that he would have the lowest score on the second half of the course.

Irv took out his mashie-niblick and began flailing away at the ball. The white egg would gain some elevation, then roll right back to where he stood. He just could not to get the thing to fly over the high grass lip and onto the green. Irv closed his eyes, said a silent prayer and gave one last hard and power strike. His iron hit low into the sand, digging beneath his ball and clanging against some old, rusting metal that sent a jarring vibration through his entire body. For a moment he thought he might faint.

Rutherford noticed how white his father-in-law had become and rushed from the green to make sure Irv was okay. "Something down there, in the sand," the former king bleated. "Something tough."

Eddie, the archeology Don, was immediately interested. "Hey, guys, give us a hand here. Let's see what Irv's sand iron struck."

Soon the others in the foursome were down in the sandy depression trying to dig the thing free, throwing the sand over the surrounding grass. "Oy, God," Irv founds himself mumbling. "Could this be the ruin of Merlin's old time machine?"

"What' that, Irv?" asked Eddie.

Irv was saved from answering by Alex, the Dean of the Literature Department. "It looks like someone's old bones are trapped in this thing, whatever it is!"

"Bones?" Rutherford questioned, "Like a skeleton?"

"What is it, anyway?" Eddie asked, leaning into the trench they'd created for a closer look.

Irv gazed on in amazement, not knowing what to say! Who would believe there was once a time machine? And if they did, what would it do to his standing in the club and the community ? Irv's son-in-law sensed the former king's discomfort with the conversation and tried to save the day. With a wink at Irv he said, "Looks like someone was trying to build some kind of mechanical dragon!"

"Thing looks quite old," stated Alex. "Rutherford old thing, didn't your paper have something to do with the history of this area? Anything about these early Jews having a mechanical dragon that ate people?" he said with a chuckle.

"I remember some news story when I was a student," Eddie, the archeology Don put in. "Some South London drug dealer that disappeared here on this very golf course. And, as I recall, they never did find his body. Maybe this old dragon rose from the ground and swallowed him up," he laughed.

"That would make a good science fiction story, if nothing else," Alex added dismissively.

"I must come back and put some students on a dig here." Eddie told the others. "Who knows what we might find." Then laughing, three members of the foursome started walking toward the next hole.

Hanging back reverently, Irv bowed his head in prayer and whispered, "Goodbye Hershel, old friend. Good to see you again. And thank you for granting my family and me a wonderful life!"

# ABOUT THE AUTHOR

Skoot Larson is a native Los Angelino, a musician, music critic and a Viet Nam veteran. He has also worked as a disc jockey, actor, speech therapist, stand-up comedian, behavioral counselor and streetcar conductor. His previous works include the Lars Lindstrom Zen-Jazz Mystery series, a black-humor novel about health care in America entitled "Apollo Issue," a political humor novel, "The Palestine Solution," and a religious comedy, "The Testament of Jessica Crystal." Skoot lives with his two cats in Rockport, Texas.

www.ingramcontent.com/pod-product-compliance
Lightning Source LLC
Chambersburg PA
CBHW031612240626
47153CB00002B/725